How long would it take before she felt completely Amish?

There must be a way to smother her past at the same time she built her future. *Then you could be the perfect Amish wife Isaac is looking for*, Rachel thought before she could halt it.

He considered her a *gut* candidate for his perfect wife, and she had to find a way to persuade him she wasn't. It'd be simple if she didn't want to protect their friendship.

She didn't want to dash his hopes as her own had been when she'd discovered her late husband's first love was his military career. She couldn't fault him. He'd never pretended to be something he wasn't.

As she was.

No! She was a plain *mamm* with two sweet daughters who wanted to help in the recovery of the flood-torn village. What she'd been in the past was in the past. What she was now was what she wanted to be in the future, but she was struggling to find her way each day.

Which made her the worst choice for Isaac to marry.

Jo Ann Brown has always loved stories with happily-ever-after endings. A former military officer, she is thrilled to have the chance to write stories about people falling in love. She is also a photographer and travels with her husband of more than thirty years to places where she can snap pictures. They have three children and live in Florida. Drop her a note at joannbrownbooks.com.

Books by Jo Ann Brown

Love Inspired

Green Mountain Blessings

An Amish Christmas Promise
An Amish Easter Wish
An Amish Mother's Secret Past

Amish Spinster Club

The Amish Suitor
The Amish Christmas Cowboy
The Amish Bachelor's Baby
The Amish Widower's Twins

Amish Hearts

Amish Homecoming
An Amish Match
His Amish Sweetheart
An Amish Reunion

Visit the Author Profile page at Harlequin.com for more titles.

An Amish Mother's Secret Past

Jo Ann Brown

LOVE INSPIRED
INSPIRATIONAL ROMANCE

LOVE INSPIRED®
INSPIRATIONAL ROMANCE

Recycling programs for this product may not exist in your area.

ISBN-13: 978-1-335-48823-7

An Amish Mother's Secret Past

Copyright © 2020 by Jo Ann Ferguson

This edition published by arrangement with Harlequin Books S.A.

For questions and comments about the quality of this book, please contact us at CustomerService@Harlequin.com.

Love Inspired
22 Adelaide St. West, 40th Floor
Toronto, Ontario M5H 4E3, Canada
www.Harlequin.com

Printed in U.S.A.

And they shall beat their swords into plowshares, and their spears into pruninghooks: nation shall not lift up sword against nation, neither shall they learn war any more.
—*Isaiah* 2:4

This is for you, Rachael.
I can't wait for the day
when you sign your first published book for me!

Chapter One

Evergreen Corners, Vermont

The day couldn't get any worse, ain't so?

Rachel Yoder prayed the answer was "no" as she pushed the stroller with her two sick *kinder* along the sidewalk edging the village green. She was supposed to be helping at the day-care center today to offset the fees for her daughters' care, but instead was taking Loribeth and Eva to the *doktor* because both were running a low-grade fever.

The little girls had been fussy from the time they'd awakened an hour before dawn. Loribeth, who was almost three years old and had hair as black as Rachel's, had her thumb in her mouth, a habit she'd given up six months ago. Rachel hadn't said anything to the toddler, because she knew sucking her thumb was giving her some comfort while she was feeling lousy. Eva, a year younger and with eyes the same warm blue as her *mamm*'s, was hunched into a pitiful ball on her side of the stroller. The September morning wasn't chilly, but the two-year-old shivered as if it was the middle of January and clutched her stuffed bear close to her. She wrapped her finger in a string from her bright blue bonnet.

Looking at them, suffering and sick, broke Rachel's heart. The pace of her steps increased as she walked across the village green. She watched for holes in the grass so the stroller didn't bounce and make the girls feel worse.

"We're almost there," she said, though she doubted the girls were paying any attention to her. They were too lost in their misery.

A few cars moved along the steep street flanking the green. The trees cast long shadows toward the western mountains, and a few leaves crunched under her black sneakers. She tilted the stroller over the curb and hurried along the sidewalk toward the center of Evergreen Corners.

The *doktor*'s office was new, having opened in mid-August. It was staffed two days a week and was affiliated with the hospital in Rutland, which was more than an hour and a half north of Evergreen Corners. The office was sandwiched between the village's diner and an antique shop on the far side of the bridge spanning Washboard Brook. The brook, which had become a torrent during the hurricane last October, was now so low that only the flattest stones were covered with water.

Traffic was busier across the bridge, so she waited for the walk light before she crossed the route that ran north and south. Hearing a moan from the stroller, Rachel paused and bent to check on her girls. They were holding hands as if trying to comfort each other. Tears filled her eyes. Their family was a small one—her and the girls since her husband's death. The tragedy had changed their lives, though she doubted the toddlers were aware of the depth of their loss yet. They simply knew their *daed* wasn't at home.

After tucking the blanket around them, she straightened. Her eyes widened when she saw someone else crossing the road. He was tall—so tall she doubted her head would top his shoulder. He wore a straw hat atop his sun-streaked caramel hair that fluttered in the breeze. She knew his eyes were the dark brown of muddy soil, though she couldn't discern that because the brim of his hat shadowed his face.

He walked toward her with his purposeful stride. It always suggested he was in the midst of something important, and everyone should get out of his way.

Isaac Kauffman was the unofficial leader of the Amish volunteers in the village. He worked under the auspices of Amish Helping Hands, the group that coordinated with plain communities to assist at disaster sites, and he had found many of the volunteers himself. She'd heard some *Englisch* volunteers call him "Mr. It's Gotta," a shortened version of "Mr. It's Gotta Be Perfectly Square." Apparently *it's gotta be perfectly square* was a phrase he used often while laying out the forms for concrete cellars. Despite their teasing, it appeared the volunteers appreciated his dedication, and he inspired everyone to make their own work match his expert foundations.

He displayed an air of arrogance few Amish men did. Her *daed* had conveyed the same silent message of believing he was better than the people around him. For his older daughter, he'd made it clear she could never meet his expectations, no matter how hard she tried. She'd struggled year after year, desperate for his approval. She'd given up and run away several times. The last time she'd jumped the fence and moved into the *Englisch* world with a vengeance.

Now…

She didn't have time to complete the thought before Isaac's path intersected hers.

"Gute mariye." His deep voice resonated like the sound of heavy machinery.

She replied to his good-morning, but other words dried in her mouth. Isaac Kauffman intimidated her, though she'd long ago vowed she wouldn't let anyone daunt her. She'd made the pledge while surrounded by loud, powerful men and women. Isaac was not loud. In the four months since his younger sister, Abby, had introduced them after Rachel's arrival in Evergreen Corners, Rachel had never once heard him raise his voice. He didn't need to. When Isaac Kauffman had something to say, everyone paused to listen. He was a man who didn't demand respect, but he received it.

In that important way, he was unlike *Daed*. She wished she could stop comparing her *daed*, Manassas Yoder, to Isaac Kauffman. She couldn't, because the aura Isaac projected raised her hackles before he said a single word. Like a *mamm* hawk, she bristled at his approach, determined to protect her young daughters from what she'd endured for too many years. She wasn't being fair to him, but she didn't care. Loribeth and Eva were too precious to her to risk them being hurt, as she'd been.

So she continued to be tongue-tied whenever she was around him. She'd found ways to avoid him or would just say a few words in passing, because she could manage a greeting, but nothing more.

Why couldn't he be more like his sister, Abby? Abby was outgoing, approachable and open, though she was as dedicated to helping as her brother was. It was difficult sometimes to remember the two were siblings. Isaac was almost ten years older than his sister. That made him about five years younger than Rachel.

"Are you heading to the community center?" Isaac asked when she didn't say anything else.

"No."

His eyebrows lowered at her terse answer, but he recovered and gave her a cool smile. "I thought you could take a message to my sister for me, but if you're not headed that way, I can—"

Loribeth threw up, spewing in Isaac's direction.

"Oh, no!" Rachel cried.

She reached to turn Loribeth away from him, but Eva began to vomit, too. The *kinder* sobbed, and their faces twisted with pain. Pulling tissues from her purse she dabbed at their gray faces. She jumped, unable to halt herself, when another round of sickness erupted from the girls. She leaned both of her *kinder* back so their lolling heads rested against the supporting wall of the stroller.

"Are they all right?" Isaac asked from behind her.

"They woke up sick this morning." Why did his simple question make her feel inadequate? "We're going to the *doktor*'s office."

"Is there anything I can do?"

She gasped when she saw his boots were covered with what had been in her daughter's stomach. *God, why did You let her throw up on Isaac Kauffman?*

It'd been accidental, she reminded herself. Isaac was being gracious, though she wondered if he'd ever had to deal with such a thing before. She couldn't imagine him—even as a little boy—getting sick on someone else. He was too exacting, never seemed to make a mistake.

Or so she'd heard the other volunteers say when they came in for meals.

She shuddered as she recalled how strict her parents

had been. Any mistake she'd made—even the simplest, most innocent one—had been deemed as dire as the most vile sin. Each was punished with lashings from a belt or by being denied meals, and each had led to her becoming more rebellious.

Don't question the reasons behind someone else's kindness, she warned herself. *Be grateful God sent help.*

Ja, that was how she must look at Isaac's unexpected assistance. As a gift from God at the moment she needed it most. Would Isaac have been solicitous if he'd known the truth about her *kinder*'s parents? How would he have reacted if he'd known that four years ago, Rachel and her late husband had been serving with the United States Army in Afghanistan?

Hearing Rachel's dismayed apology, Isaac looked at his splattered boots. "Don't worry. I can assure you they've been covered in worse."

He'd hoped Rachel would laugh at his jest, but she kept saying how sorry she was. Never before had he heard her string so many words together. Abby had assured him Rachel wasn't shy around everyone, and that she chattered like an eager squirrel while working in the community center where the volunteers took their meals. She'd always been quiet in his company.

He wanted to put his hands on her shoulders and urge her to calm herself. Her *bopplin* were screwing up their adorable, pudgy faces, and he didn't want three females crying in front of him. He knew too well how *kinder* could be, because he'd raised his younger brothers and sister after their *mamm* died and *Daed* had sought consolation in the bottom of a bottle he thought Isaac didn't know he kept hidden in the barn.

Isaac had met Rachel several times at the community

center's kitchen. She had the blackest hair he'd ever seen, without a hint of silver, though she looked to be in her middle thirties, around his age. The color was as if the night sky had been stripped of its stars, but their glow had been left behind. When she glanced at him as she tried to clean her *kinder*, he realized her eyes were almost the same vivid blue as the sheen of September sunlight on the hair in front of her pleated, box-shaped *kapp*.

Her face, however, was almost as colorless as her *kinder*'s. Was she ill, too?

"Can I help?" he asked.

"No!" She sounded as appalled at the idea as she had when her little girl had thrown up on his boots. She squared her shoulders, then added, "*Danki*, Isaac, but that's not necessary. I know you're busy. Like I said, we're on our way to the *doktor*, and he'll give them something to settle their stomachs."

"I'll pray for quick healing for them."

"I'm sure it's some twenty-four-hour bug, but their fevers worry me. *Danki* for offering. Again, I'm sorry—"

"It's okay, Rachel." He bent toward the stroller to tuck in an end of the blanket covering the *kinder*.

He froze when he looked into eyes as deep a brown as his own. The words he'd been about to say, that he wished Rachel and her little ones well, disappeared when he saw the entreaty in the older girl's eyes. Why was the *kind* looking at him like that? She didn't know him.

Sorrow pinched him as he remembered hearing the *kinder*'s *daed* was dead, leaving his pretty widow with two *bopplin*. Did the little girl long for a man to comfort her when she was ill? Did the *kind* remember her *daed*?

He sighed. Though there had been many years when he'd wished his *daed* had been different, he wouldn't have traded a single day with him. *Daed* had remarried and given up drinking. The jovial man Isaac recalled from his youth was back. It was a treasured gift, one these little girls would never experience because their *daed* wouldn't return.

"Is there something else, Isaac?"

At Rachel's question, he realized he'd been lost too long in his thoughts. Standing straighter, he said, "Let me walk with you to the *doktor*'s office."

"That's not necessary."

"If they start throwing up, you may need help."

When she hesitated, he couldn't help wondering if he'd done something to offend her.

Learn to do well; seek judgment, relieve the oppressed, judge the fatherless, plead for the widow. The verse from the first chapter of Isaiah rang through his mind. It was one he'd learned from his mentor, Clyde Felter, when he was a boy and had followed Clyde around while the wizened mason taught him how to work with stone and concrete. Clyde had liked to quote Scripture, and his favorite verses had to do with helping those who were in need.

If Clyde had been standing beside him, the old man would have insisted Isaac do what was right. What was right, Isaac knew, was overruling Rachel's polite refusal for his assistance.

Isaac took the stroller's handle and motioned for Rachel to lead the way to the *doktor*'s office. She didn't move for a long moment, then nodded. *Gut!* She could be sensible. He chided himself for his impatience. She was anxious about her *kinder*'s health. What a *gut mamm* she was!

The type of *mamm* he hoped to have for his *kinder* when he was able to purchase a farm and settle down with a wife and family. He pushed aside that thought. His family still needed his assistance at their farm in northeast Vermont. His youngest brother, Herman, should be taking over soon, and then Isaac could move ahead with his plans.

As they walked over the bridge, Isaac glanced at the buildings on either side of the street. Most near the brook had been damaged during the flood, but only the massive brick factory building remained closed. It was scheduled to open next month, almost a year after Hurricane Kevin had sent a wall of water crashing through the village. To the north, along a slow curve in Washboard Brook, he could see the half skeleton of the covered bridge. It wouldn't be rebuilt soon because the list of bridges needing repair or replacement in central Vermont was long. Fortunately, the highway bridge in the center of town had been repaired.

When Rachel paused by what once must have been a private home, which was set in the shadow of a huge Victorian with an antique store on the main floor, he saw the plaque announcing the small building housed the Evergreen Corners Medical Clinic. The white cottage had dark green shutters with silhouettes of pine trees cut into them. The front door was a welcoming red and had a wreath decorated with fake thermometers and tongue depressors hanging on it.

Putting her hand on the stroller and drawing it toward the door, Rachel said, "*Danki* for coming with us, Isaac. You've been kind."

"We help one another."

She flinched at his answer, and he realized it had been more curt than he intended. How often had his sister warned him he needed to be more aware of his tone when he spoke to others? Abby could discern his true feelings in spite of how his words sounded, but he'd been a part of her life since she was born.

He reached to open the door, and Rachel checked her daughters before she tipped the stroller over the threshold. She couldn't hide her amazement when he followed her into the office. Had she expected him to leave her with two sick *kinder*? When she looked away without saying anything, he guessed she'd come to accept that he intended to do as he said.

The *doktor*'s office appeared empty. No patients waited on the half-dozen plastic chairs arranged along the walls. Posters with health information decorated the light green walls. Opposite the front door, a half wall was topped by frosted glass.

A window in the glass wall slid open. "Can I help you?"

Isaac said, "Go ahead. I'll watch your girls."

Rachel hurried along a bright blue section of the tile floor to the half wall. Her voice was hushed as she spoke with the gray-haired woman who sat on the other side of the window.

Rocking the stroller as she had, he listened while Rachel gave her name as well as the *kinder*'s and explained why she was there.

"Oh, the poor dears," the woman said. "There's a nasty bug going around, and it seems to like the little ones the most. The doctor has just arrived from Rutland." She smiled. "He was delayed by the birth of triplets this morning. Please take a seat, and I'll call you in as soon as he's ready to see you."

Isaac chose a chair and watched as Rachel kneeled next to the stroller. She drew some wet wipes from her black purse and dabbed them along the little girls' faces.

They moaned, and he was glad he'd stayed. It had been the right thing to do.

He knew Glen Landis, the project manager overseeing the plain volunteers in Evergreen Corners, would understand why Isaac was late for their scheduled meeting. Glen would be leaving the town at the end of the year along with most of the aid organizations. A new project manager would be appointed, if necessary. Isaac had heard rumors he would be offered the job, but Glen hadn't mentioned anything to him.

If offered, would he take it? It didn't fit in with the plans he had for his life, but how could he walk away when so much remained to be done in Evergreen Corners?

A door to the right of the half wall opened, and a man stepped out. The *doktor*, who wore a red-and-white-striped shirt and blue jeans under his white medical coat, was a short, rotund man with a pair of gold-rimmed glasses perched on top of his bald head.

"Mrs. Yoder?" the *doktor* asked with a reassuring smile. "I hear the stomach bug has come to your house."

"Ja." She stood and faced him. "Are you ready for us?"

"Whenever you're ready. Let's see what we can do to make these two youngsters more comfortable." When she started toward the door, the *doktor* looked at Isaac. "Why don't you come in, too? It'll be simpler with two sick children to have both parents there."

"Isaac isn't their *daed*." A bright pink flashed up Rachel's cheeks. "He's a… He's a…"

"I'm a fellow volunteer in town," Isaac said quickly. "Isaac Kauffman."

"I see." The *doktor* hooked a thumb at the door. "If

you don't mind volunteering right now, Isaac, it'll make the exam easier for everyone."

Standing, he nodded. The *doktor* walked through the doorway, and Rachel followed, pushing the stroller. She didn't turn her head in time for him to miss her expression. She wasn't happy about him coming into the examination room. He'd stuck his nose in where it didn't belong with no more excuse than her *kind* had thrown up on his boots. He'd have to find a way to apologize later.

The *doktor* was washing his hands when Isaac joined Rachel and her daughters in the examination room. Like the waiting room, the walls were covered with posters. A table topped by a paper sheet dominated the room, and three plastic chairs were set along the wall.

"I'm Dr. Kingsley." He dried his hands and walked to the examination table. "What's wrong with these cuties, Mom?"

"They're running a slight fever," Rachel replied. She pointed to each *kind* as she spoke their names. "Loribeth, the older one, had a temperature of one hundred point two, and Eva had ninety-nine point eight."

"Any other symptoms? Fussiness? Coughing? Vomiting?"

"All of them."

The *doktor* glanced at Isaac, his gaze slipping to Isaac's boots. "Ah, so I see."

"I wasn't quick enough to get out of the way," Isaac said, annoyed at the *doktor*'s jesting tone.

"No one can be fast enough to escape every time." Dr. Kingsley motioned for Rachel to put Loribeth on the exam table and for her to remove the *kinder*'s dress. Picking up his stethoscope, he said, "My oldest once stood at the top of the stairs and vomited. She hit every step. My wife and I were grateful we'd pulled out the old carpet days before." After warming the stethoscope between his palms, he cupped it so Loribeth could examine it.

The little girl ignored him, whining and holding up her arms to her *mamm* in a wordless request for comfort. Rachel soothed the little girl but glanced at the stroller as the other *kind* began crying. Raising her remarkable eyes, she shot Isaac a pleading glance.

Hoping he remembered the skills he'd learned when his siblings were tiny, he unlatched the straps holding the toddler in the stroller and scooped her up. She retched, and he steeled himself, but she didn't throw up. He cradled the *kind* until the *doktor* had finished examining her sister.

While Rachel held Loribeth, he put Eva on the table and stepped back to let Dr. Kingsley check her, as well. He was pleased to hear the *doktor* announce the *kinder* were fine except for the stomach bug. He prescribed something to ease their cramps and help them sleep.

"If they're feeling better tomorrow," Dr. Kingsley said, "and I suspect they will be, you can discontinue the medicine. However, they're contagious. You all are. You should go home and stay away from other people until at least tomorrow. If you don't have any symptoms by noon tomorrow, you shouldn't be able to pass along the germs any longer."

Isaac bit back his groan. He was supposed to be finishing the preparations for a new foundation today. "If I'm working outdoors, will being around other people be a problem?"

"It won't be a problem as long as you don't breathe around them or touch anything they touch." The *doktor* gave him a regretful smile. "I know it's difficult, but the best way to avoid this spreading is to stay away from others for twenty-four to thirty-six hours. I suspect we'll be seeing more children from the day-care center today and tomorrow."

Accepting the inevitable, Isaac stood to one side as Rachel dressed her *kinder*. She thanked the *doktor* and put the girls into the stroller with Isaac's help. As soon as they were on the street, she began to apologize again.

"It's not your fault, Rachel. God decided I need a day off. I'll spend the time doing the paperwork Glen has been after me to complete. It's better I skip a day than infect everyone else."

When he asked if she needed help getting the *kinder* home, she shook her head and thanked him as she walked away.

He watched her push the stroller along the sidewalk. Odd. He hadn't paid much attention to her until this morning. He'd noticed her, of course, because she was a lovely woman and a dedicated volunteer.

Maybe he should have looked more closely. He'd turned thirty-five and no longer had the obligations he'd had for the years when his *daed* had been impaired by alcohol. It was time to find the perfect wife. He wasn't seeking a great romance. His heart, he knew, was too practical.

He'd escorted plenty of girls home in his courting buggy when he was a teenager. Not once had he been interested—nor had they—in him taking them home a second time. As he grew older, the pool of available women had lessened in their district and the neighboring ones in Lancaster County before his family moved north. His hope he'd find his match waiting for him in northern Vermont hadn't worked out, either.

He knew what he wanted in a wife. An excellent cook. A *wunderbaar mamm* for their *kinder*. A hard worker who wouldn't hesitate to join him in making the farm he intended to buy a success. Someone who loved animals. A woman of deep faith.

As Rachel crossed the road, heading away from him, he smiled. He'd seen that she fit one of his criteria. She was a dedicated *mamm*. What about his other requirements for a perfect Amish wife? Did she meet them?

It could be, he decided, time for him to find out.

Chapter Two

Rachel sat on the edge of the low tub and watched her girls splashing in the warm water. As the *doktor* had assured her, the medicine had settled their stomachs since morning, and their temperatures were almost normal. Keeping an eye on them as they pushed an inflatable fish between them, she reached for another towel to drape across the floor where water puddled beside the tub. It was so *gut* to see her daughters feeling better she didn't mind the mess.

She leaned against the wall behind her. The trailer Rachel and her *kinder* called home was set on a knoll not far from the high school. The mobile home's owner had made the space available for volunteers, in gratitude for their help in repairing his *mamm*'s house soon after the flood. The few pieces of furniture in the cramped spaces were cast-offs, but some generous soul had found two small beds because her girls were too young to sleep in the bunks that had been in the bedroom. Those bunks had been sent to someone else to use. She could barely squeeze between the two beds, but her daughters were happy sharing a room.

In the kitchen, the dishes had chips and scrapes, but

everything was usable. With most of their possessions in storage, the setup was perfect. Rachel had room to cook and not much to keep clean. The backyard, though it sloped toward the high school, was fenced so she could let the girls play outside while she watched them through one of the trailer's many windows.

When Glen had arranged for them to live in the mobile home, the project manager couldn't have known how much the place would remind her of her earliest days in family housing on various Army posts after she'd married Travis Gauthier. Simple, small rooms with white walls and well-used cabinetry.

Her lips tightened, and she stiffened as she did whenever she thought about the life she'd left behind after Travis died when his truck hit an improvised explosive device. Nobody must know the truth about her past. A long time ago, when she'd run away from home for the last time, so she could escape being forced to marry a young man she detested, she'd found what she thought was the place she was meant to be. She'd joined the Army, becoming a transportation officer and serving around the world. A small whisper in her mind had urged her to reconsider, but she'd muted that voice until after Travis's death.

As she searched for what she'd do as a widow with two young *kinder* and no ties anywhere, she hadn't been able to ignore the voice and the longing within her to be closer to God. She'd moved as far as possible from her former district in Ohio and been welcomed into another community in Maine. Her new neighbors had assumed she'd been baptized as Amish, and they'd accepted her as one of them. For the six months she'd lived among them, she'd made every effort not to say or do anything to make them question their assumption.

Yet, living among the *Leit* under false pretenses had gnawed at her, so when the chance came to help with rebuilding Evergreen Corners, she'd volunteered. In the small town, she was able to straddle the plain and *Englisch* worlds as she had for the past twenty years. She hoped while she worked alongside other volunteers, her prayers for guidance about the future would be answered. She could accept being ostracized from the plain community for her choices, but she didn't want her little girls to have to pay the price. There must be a way to do as God wanted and return to the Amish and be baptized. She had to wait for God to show her the path.

The doorbell rang, breaking into Rachel's thoughts. She looked at her girls as the bell sounded again.

If she grabbed towels and wrapped them around her daughters, she could carry one in each arm to the front door. It'd been a rainy afternoon, and she didn't want to risk them getting chilled while she answered the door.

Never taking her eyes off the girls, she stretched so she could shout down the hall. She used the voice she'd perfected in the motor pool when she had to get everyone's attention over the cacophony of tools and loud voices and parts hitting the concrete floor.

"*Komm* in!"

Eva got water in her eyes and began to cry. Rachel distracted her with another inflatable fish, allowing her to dab away the teardrops. The little girl began to giggle.

"Is she all right?"

At the question from behind her, Rachel flinched so hard she nearly tumbled into the tub. A broad hand on her arm steadied her at the same time it sent warmth swirling along her skin.

She looked over her shoulder, though she didn't need

to. The deep voice told her Isaac stood in her bathroom doorway.

What was *he* doing here?

Her fingers were patting her hair toward her *kapp* before she could halt herself. She didn't like the feeling that it was impossible for her to live up to his high standards. It'd be simpler if she wasn't trying to persuade everyone she was no different from any other Amish widow. She didn't want anyone asking questions about her past.

When he removed his black hat, his light brown hair was tousled. Rachel was surprised that it wasn't as perfectly trained as the rest of him. She silently scolded herself. She was being petty.

"They're fine," she said.

"So my boots are safe?" he asked.

"Ja." Embarrassment warmed her face, and her cheeks must have been scarlet. She couldn't remember the last time she'd blushed. "If you want to wait in the other room, I'll have them out of the tub soon."

"Let me help."

She was so astonished she blurted the first stupid thing that came into her head. "They're wet."

"The usual situation when a *kind* is in the bathtub."

Okay, she had to wonder why he wanted to talk to her when she'd acted ridiculous. Without further comment, she handed him a towel from the floor, one that wasn't as wet as the others. She picked up another and lifted Eva from the tub, wrapping her in soft plushness. She watched as Isaac did the same with Loribeth, who regarded him with big eyes.

"Don't wiggle," he said in *Deitsch*, the language he would assume the girls spoke. Most Amish *kinder*, especially those without older siblings, didn't learn to speak like *Englischers* until they started school when they were six years old.

"Who are you?" the little girl asked in the same language, and Rachel released a silent sigh of relief.

"My name is Isaac."

"I-zak?" Her nose wrinkled. "That's a funny name. My name is pretty. It's Loribeth."

"Did the bath make you feel better, Loribeth?"

"Pudding makes me feel *gut*." She regarded him with a serious expression. "Chocolate pudding."

"I think," he said with a wink at the little girl, "chocolate makes everyone feel *gut*."

"Choco!" Eva crowed, bouncing in Rachel's arms. "Yummy! Choco puddin'?"

"Not now," Rachel said. "You need to brush your teeth and go to bed."

"Choco puddin' for break-ist?"

"How about you and Loribeth help me make chocolate pudding tomorrow for supper?"

Both girls tried not to appear too disappointed as they nodded. When they looked at each other and giggled, she shook her head. They were young, but she suspected they'd already learned to work together to get what they wanted from their *mamm*.

Isaac held Eva, once Rachel had put on her diaper and nightgown, while Rachel got Loribeth ready for bed. The littler girl wore diapers at night. Rachel glanced in Isaac's direction to see if he'd taken note of the fact her younger daughter wasn't completely potty-trained, but his expression told her nothing. Hurrying made her fingers clumsy, and Loribeth complained when Rachel pulled her nightgown over her head backward.

Rachel twisted it around and buttoned the front. As Loribeth scrambled into her small bed, Rachel lifted Eva onto hers. She listened while the little girls said their heartfelt prayers and kissed them as she tucked them under the covers.

She turned to pick up the wet towels and was startled to discover Isaac already had. She hadn't noticed him leaving the room. Forcing her jaw to ease from its taut line, she was able to smile when Eva called her name.

"Med-y?" asked the toddler.

With a genuine smile, Rachel shook her head. "You don't need any more medicine. The *doktor* said once your tummies were okay, you didn't need to take any more. You and Loribeth are *gut*, so no more medicine."

"Gut." Eva settled into her pillow, pulling her beloved *Boppli* Bear against her chest.

Rachel drew a blanket over her younger daughter, though Eva would kick it off. The little girl hated having anything on her when she was sleeping. Soon Rachel would have to open the boxes with the girls' winter clothing and find Loribeth's old pajamas for her younger sister.

After turning to make sure Loribeth was set for the night, she saw a puzzled expression on the little girl's face. "What is it, *liebling*?" she asked.

"I don't like that I-zak."

"You don't know him." She hadn't expected to have to defend the man who unsettled her, but her daughters must not do anything to draw attention to the fact they hadn't always lived plain. She guessed no Amish *kind* would speak so about an adult.

"Don't want to know him."

"Loribeth, that's not what God asks of us. We're supposed to be friends to everyone."

"Not *him*." She turned her back on Rachel, making it clear she didn't want to discuss Isaac any longer.

Rachel turned off the ceiling light, made sure the two

night-lights were on and slipped out of the room, drawing the door almost closed. Was her daughter going to be as rebellious as Rachel had been as a teen?

She must find out why Isaac had come to the trailer and walked in as if he owned the place.

Because you told him to. She couldn't ignore the honest voice in her mind. She *had* asked Isaac to *komm* in, though she hadn't imagined he was the person knocking on her door.

Rachel paused at the end of the short hallway leading to the compact kitchen. Isaac stood in front of the sofa in the living room as if he couldn't imagine sitting without permission.

"Isaac, *danki*." She bit her lip. Isaac had been annoyed earlier when she'd thanked him over and over. "I appreciate your help in getting the girls out of the tub."

"They seem to be feeling better."

"They are. I've stopped the medicine because they were able to keep ginger ale and crackers down this evening."

He motioned toward a pot from a slow cooker sitting in the middle of the dining table. A dishcloth covered the top. "My sister sent some chicken soup over. She said you'd know when to give it to the *kinder*."

"I'm sure they'll appreciate it tomorrow."

"Not as much as *choco puddin'*, I would guess."

Was that a hint of a smile she saw on his face? Was he amused by the girls, or did he think her parenting skills were a joke?

"If Eva had her way, she'd have pudding for every meal every day." Hoping he wasn't wondering where her manners were, she added, "I made a cake before the girls got sick. I put it in the freezer, but I could warm it if you'd like a piece."

"Sure."

"You don't care what flavor it is?"

"I've never been offered a piece of cake I didn't like." He gave her another of his rare smiles as they went into the kitchen.

The owner had told her the appliances were a color called avocado-green, but if she had an avocado that dull, she would have tossed it, unsure if it was safe to eat. Walking to the stove, she asked, *"Kaffi?"*

"It's late, so I shouldn't." He started to say more, but halted when another knock came at her door.

Startled, because she couldn't remember the last time she'd had anyone drop by in the evening since her arrival in Evergreen Corners, let alone two visitors, Rachel hurried to the door. She opened it and gasped, "Abby! What are you doing here? Oh, that was rude!"

"Not at all." Abby's smile was easy.

Isaac's sister's hair was as blond as the streaks in his, but they were otherwise opposites in appearance. She was short while he was tall, and her eyes were a greenish-gray instead of the earth-brown of his. However, they were eager volunteers. From what Rachel had been told, Abby had come to the village within weeks of the flood and had remained in Evergreen Corners to oversee the kitchen in the community center, where the volunteers were fed three meals a day. In addition, she'd taken on working with the teenage volunteers in an effort to curtail bullying in the village. Her efforts, like her brother's, had been successful. However, unlike Isaac, Abby asked of others only what they could give.

"I'm the one who's being rude," Abby said as she stepped into the trailer. "I couldn't wait for Isaac to come home and tell me. How are the girls?"

"Asleep, I hope. I put them to bed after a warm bath."

"That's *gut*." She glanced toward the kitchen. "I hope Isaac isn't being too much of a bossy bother."

"No!" Rachel lowered her voice. "He's trying to help."

"He doesn't *try*. He does everything perfectly." She smiled. "I love my brother, but I don't make excuses for him."

Rachel decided she'd be wise not to say anything in response. "*Danki* for sending over the soup."

"I'm glad I can help. I figured they'd be ready for real food soon." She chuckled. "Unlike the kids in the youth group, who are ready for food at any time and at any place."

Joining in with her soft laughter, Rachel's uncertainties were alleviated when Abby agreed to have some cake, too. Rachel went into the kitchen and hoped Abby's presence would ease the tension between herself and Isaac. It wasn't much of a defensive plan, but it was the best she had at the moment.

The morning sunshine sifted through the leaves on the tree outside the window of the apartment where Isaac lived with his sister when he was in southern Vermont. The apartment was over a garage belonging to the mayor of Evergreen Corners, Gladys Whittaker, and her husband. From the moment the space had been offered to Isaac and Abby, it had become his home away from home. Abby wouldn't be returning to live at the family farm in the Northeast Kingdom because she was going to marry, but he'd been traveling back and forth every couple of weeks. He'd ridden with other volunteers in the rented van so many times along the mountain roads he felt as if he could drive them blindfolded.

Not that he knew how to drive a car. When his friends, during their *rumspringa*, had gotten licenses, he hadn't.

He'd intended to commit himself to an Amish life, and he hadn't needed a taste of everything that would be forbidden to him once he was baptized. Instead of a fast car, he'd spent his time listening to the radio he'd hidden in the hayloft, along with a few comic books that would have earned him a long lecture if *Daed* had discovered them. As his *daed* spent most of those years sneaking alcohol from his stash in the barn, Isaac had been extra careful to keep his contraband out of sight. He'd thought nobody had known about his stash until a few months ago, when Abby told him she'd found his comic books and had read them. She'd been delighted, as he had, by the outrageous stories of people who could fly and see through buildings and spent their lives fighting evil.

This morning, he wasn't reading about the adventures of a superhero. Instead, he was perusing the local newspaper as he finished his cold *kaffi*. *The Evergreen Corners Crier* was published weekly. Front-page news focused on events at the high school, and the inside pages were filled with birth announcements, obituaries and menus for the senior centers in the neighboring towns. The Evergreen Corners seniors had met at the community center before the flood and now shared the space with the volunteers, who depended on the kitchen for their meals.

He'd scanned those stories, but his attention had been riveted on the classified section. A single picture showed a fuzzy image of a weathered barn and a house. The photo had run in the paper each week for the past three months as part of a real-estate ad. The copy spoke of eighty acres, more than twenty wooded. The property had been a dairy farm.

Leaning back in his chair, Isaac looked around the apartment's kitchen, which was barely larger than the one in Rachel's trailer. What would the kitchen look like in the battered old house? It probably was large enough for a family and could be the heart of the home he hoped to share with a wife and their *kinder*.

"Gute mariye," Abby sang out as she came into the kitchen. Earlier, as she did each morning, she'd made a hearty breakfast for them before she went to the community center to do the same for whoever needed a meal before the day's work began.

Isaac's dream popped like a soap bubble, and he closed the newspaper, not wanting his sister to guess he was mooning over the farm outside of the village.

Too late, he realized, when Abby said, "You should go and look before someone else buys it."

"It's been for sale for a long time. I don't think anyone's interested in it."

"You are." She chuckled as she added more detergent to the water in the sink so she could finish the dishes.

"Our family lives almost three hours north of here. Why would I be looking at farms here?"

She shot a sugary smile in his direction. "Because your favorite sister lives here."

"My *only* sister."

"But your favorite, you've got to admit."

Part of him wanted to give in to Abby's silliness, but he had too much on his mind. The farm, the work ahead of him…two little girls and their *mamm*. God had brought them into his life. Why?

Abby scrubbed the pan she'd used to make them pancakes. "It wouldn't hurt for you to contact the real-estate agent. She's right here in town. I'm sure she'd be glad to show you around the farm."

"I'm sure she would, but I don't want to waste her time when I'm not ready to buy."

"Why not? You know more about running a farm than

anyone else in the family. Even *Daed* isn't as skilled a dairyman as you are!"

"A farmer needs more than himself to make the farm successful."

"You may be able to hire older teen boys to help with haying and harvest."

"Harvest comes at the same time as preseason football practice."

Her eyebrows rose. "Wow, you've given this some thought, haven't you?"

"A lot."

"So what's keeping you from seeing the farm?"

"I told you. I'm not ready."

She gave an unattractive snort. His sister never hid her opinions around him. "I know you, Isaac Kauffman! You hate wasting time, but yet you're acting like a boy dreaming of a new baseball glove. You should visit the farm. It's not far from the Millers' house, which would be convenient for church Sundays."

"That's true."

"So why aren't you going to look at the farm?"

She wouldn't give up until he was honest with her. Completely honest.

"A farmer should have a wife and family to help him."

Abby put the skillet into the sink. With soap suds clinging to her fingers, she faced him and said, "So I guess that means you're looking for a wife. I could say it's about time. You're thirty-five, and most men have been married for years by the time they're your age."

"I haven't found the woman I want to spend the rest of my life with."

"You haven't found the *perfect* woman, you mean." She laughed as she turned back to the sink. "I know you, big brother. You want everything perfect."

"Why shouldn't I?"

"What about falling in love? I haven't heard you say a word about that."

"Love isn't all it's touted to be." What was the use of love when it had driven his *daed* to drinking and almost torn apart their family? "Let me find what I'm looking for, Abby, without your help. I didn't get involved when you found the perfect man for yourself."

"Really?" She arched her eyebrows.

"Okay, I didn't get involved as much as I wanted to."

"That's likely true." She smiled. "I didn't find the perfect man. I've found the right man, and I know we'll be happy when we marry after he's baptized. Right and perfect aren't the same thing."

"They are for me."

"Isaac, you know as well as I do there's only one perfect being—God. How can you expect a mortal woman to achieve a state of perfection?"

"You're arguing over a single word. When I say perfect, I mean perfect for me. Why shouldn't I want that?"

Instead of the pert, teasing answer he'd thought she'd give him, his sister became serious as she looked over her shoulder. "Because you may miss the right woman for you while waiting for the perfect one to come along. I hope you don't make that mistake, Isaac."

He hoped so, too.

Chapter Three

The day-care center, Rachel knew, had been at the community center for almost five months after the flood. Once Reverend Rhee, the retired minister, had moved out of the church basement and into the new house Amish Helping Hands had built for her, the day-care center had returned to its original location at the Evergreen Corners Community Church. While it had moved back almost six months ago, Rachel smiled as she thought of how excited everyone involved had been to have the day-care center once more in the basement of the small white church. It had been seen as another step toward returning the village to what it had been before the storm. The *kinder* had been delighted to go to their familiar classrooms along with their toys and teachers.

Voices reached them as she went with her daughters down the uncarpeted stairs to the cellar, glad to be out of the rain. The bright colors of the classrooms seemed more garish after the dull gray of the early morning.

"Look who's back!" called Gwen O'Malley, the head teacher, as she smiled at the girls, who gripped Rachel's hands. She was a slender woman with a moon-shaped face. A curly red cloud topped her head, and was always flopping about like the stuffed arms and legs of Eva's bear. She adored *kinder*, and they returned her affection. Both girls flung their short arms around her and began chattering.

"How are you feeling, Loribeth? Eva?" the woman they called "Miss Gwen" asked. "Are your tummies happy?"

Loribeth rubbed her stomach. "It ouched." She'd switched to English easily.

"Ouched," Eva said, echoing her older sister.

"I know." Gwen squatted in front of them. "Your tummies don't ouch now, do they?"

Both girls shook their heads so seriously Rachel had to struggle not to grin. Gwen's lips twitched, too.

"I threw up on I-zak's boots," Loribeth said, telling the story with the drama of a telenovela actress. "He got me out of the tub, but Mommy put me to bed." She couldn't hide her delight that she'd messed up Isaac's boots.

Later, Rachel would have to remind Loribeth that being nice to others, even people her daughter disliked, was important. As she listened to her girls, she wondered why she'd worried. They'd been in Evergreen Corners since the spring, so it would have been bizarre if the girls weren't speaking English while among the town's residents.

Fretting wasn't like her. She'd learned in the Army to have a clear vision of her goals, but her brain hadn't contained many intelligible thoughts since Travis's death. On the day when a knock on her door had signaled the arrival of the local post chaplain, logic had deserted her.

How could there be any logic in a world where her husband and the *daed* of her *kinder* had been killed in the final week of his deployment?

Sorrow flooded her, threatening to drown her in the memories of the *gut* times and plans for the future that would never come to pass. She silenced the thoughts, refusing to let them escape from where she'd locked them away in her heart. She wished she could have buried them along with her husband, as rifles had fired a salute and she'd accepted the folded American flag along with the gratitude of the American people. Knowing the Army was the most important thing in Travis's life had offered her some comfort because he'd died doing what he loved. Yet, she wished he could see how much the girls had grown. He'd missed Loribeth's first words and every milestone Eva had made.

"Right, Mommy?"

At Eva's voice, she escaped the quicksand of her memories. She found a smile and pasted it in place as she stroked her daughter's hair. Not wanting to admit she hadn't heard anything her girls or Gwen had said, she smiled. "I need to get to work, *lieblings*. Be *gut* for Miss Gwen."

She gave them each a kiss and watched as they loped over to where other *kinder* had gathered to listen to a story. There were fewer than half of the normal number of *kinder* in the room.

As if Rachel had spoken aloud, Gwen said, "We've got a bunch of kids out with the stomach bug. It's going through the staff, too."

"Do you need me to help today?"

Gwen smiled. "Thanks, Rachel, but we're okay at the moment, and I know today is your day to work in the kitchen. Go ahead. We'll be fine."

"If you need me, call the community center and I'll come right over."

"I appreciate that, but I hope I won't have to chase you down."

"Me, either." With a wave, Rachel climbed the stairs and went out the door into the soggy September morning.

She bent her head into the rain, drawing her black cloak over her bonnet, though it was too warm for the heavy garment. When bringing her girls to day care, it was easier to drape a cloak over them rather than try to squeeze beneath an umbrella.

Hearing shouts from the other side of the village green, she watched as a group of men strode north toward the latest building sites. She could pick out Isaac easily. He walked with a steady pace, his head high. The small matter of rain didn't keep Isaac Kauffman from moving forward with his day.

It shouldn't hold her back, either. Bowing her head into the wind, she scurried toward the community center set next to the Mennonite chapel. Water splashed out of puddles and dropped off trees. Her sneakers and black stockings were soaked by the time she threw open the door and rushed inside.

The main room of the community center was filled with tables and assorted chairs that had been donated eleven months ago, after the flood. Other than the volunteers, only a handful of local villagers continued to take their meals at the community center. Those people would be able to make meals in their own kitchens once the last three houses under construction were finished. In the months since the flood, twelve houses had been built, after the debris left by the high water had been trucked away.

Breakfast had been under way for at least an hour, but fresh food awaited any stragglers at the pass-through window between the main room and the kitchen. After she'd taken off her cloak and black bonnet and hung them near the door, Rachel ignored the stack of cranberry muffins and hurried into the kitchen.

It was warm and smelled of bacon and eggs from breakfast. Two women were cutting freshly baked bread in preparation for making lunch sandwiches. Two others were loading the dishwasher while another cleaned pans in the sink. Abby was taking meats, lettuce and tomatoes from the refrigerator, and carrying them to a counter.

Rachel took a steadying breath. The kitchen was more crowded than usual. She saw two new workers. The one cutting bread was a tall blonde who wore a heart-shaped *kapp* above a lovely face. The other was an *Englischer* whose light brown hair was cut into a bob. She was a couple of inches taller than Rachel, and she moved around the kitchen in a flurry of energy as she stacked dirty dishes in the dishwasher.

Calling a greeting, Abby set the food on the counter and came over to introduce Rachel to the newcomers. The tall blonde was Nina Streit from eastern Lancaster County. Her voice complemented her beauty. Her curves couldn't be hidden by the simple dress she wore beneath a black apron.

"So glad you've joined us," Rachel said.

The tall woman bowed her head, then went back to work.

Abby turned toward the shorter woman. "Rachel, I don't think you've met Hailee Lennox. Hailee, this is Rachel Yoder."

"So glad you've joined us, too." Rachel steeled herself for another cool reaction.

Instead, Hailee said, "Me, too! The folks here are nice. I'm glad I finally got a chance to come and join in." She grinned. "I can come a couple of days a week and on the weekends when I'm not training with my National Guard unit."

Rachel looked away, hoping her face didn't display her shock at meeting another female soldier. Her eyes were caught by Nina's. The tall woman regarded her with a curious expression and a half smile, as if she'd guessed Rachel's secret.

Don't be silly. Her secret was safe.

Moving her gaze to Abby, she asked, "What do you need me to do this morning?"

"Cupcakes."

"Sounds like fun."

"Why don't you have Hailee help you? You can teach her how we do things here."

Glad that Abby had asked her to help Hailee instead of icy Nina, Rachel was soon busy showing Hailee where to find the ingredients for the cupcakes they'd serve with lunch. On such a stormy day, warm dessert would be welcomed by the volunteers. They were stirring batter when Nina moved to join them.

"How long have you been here, Rachel?" she asked as she began greasing and flouring the cupcake pans.

"Since spring."

"So long?"

"*Ja.* I'll be staying as long as I'm needed here."

Nina's eyebrows rose. "My family expects me home by the end of October. I have two sisters and a brother getting married, so they want the whole family there. How about yours?"

Abby paused on the other side of the prep table, and Rachel was grateful when her friend asked, "Have you seen the insulated container for *kaffi*?"

"I have." Glad she didn't have to answer Nina's question, Rachel went to the pantry across from the stoves. She'd met people like Nina before—people who had to establish a pecking order with themselves at the top. The best way to deal with them, she'd learned, was to avoid any competition with them.

Opening the door to the walk-in pantry, she stood on tiptoe to reach the blue-and-white plastic jug they used to send hot or cold drinks to the volunteers on the work sites. Her fingertips touched it, but she couldn't get her hands around it. Not wanting to bother getting a chair to stand on, she jumped and tapped one side of the container. She smiled when the jug moved an inch closer. It was enough for her to be able to pull it off the shelf.

A sharp crash sounded behind her. She gripped the insulated jug to her chest and whirled. A scream burst from her throat before she could halt it. Had that been gunfire? A bomb going off? The unforgettable odors of sweat and blood and heat surged over her, and she pressed against the pantry wall.

The pantry!

She was in Evergreen Corners, Vermont. She was—

Her eyes widened when she saw everyone in the kitchen had halted. The women stared at her in dismay. No wonder. She must look like a *dummkopf* cowering in the pantry. If they had any idea of the images rushing through her mind…

They must never know. She had to keep the truth to herself.

Horror rushed through her, wiping away every other thought, when a motion on the other side of the pass-through window caught her eye. Isaac stood there. His face was rigid. Somehow she had to make sure any suspicions he might have were quickly allayed.

Isaac scanned the tableau in front of him. Beside him, Vernon Umble, his cousin, stared through his thick glasses that were, as always, perched on the tip of his nose. The volunteers in the kitchen were as still as statues. They were all looking at where Rachel stood in the door to the pantry. Her face was empty of color, and though she was struggling to smile, he couldn't miss the remnants of fear in her eyes. He wouldn't insult her by assuming she'd been startled by a mouse. She was made of much sterner stuff.

So what had made her scream as if she was afraid for her life?

Rachel straightened and smiled, but he guessed it was forced. "Sorry! I was startled by the crash."

"I dropped a cookie sheet," said Abby.

"The noise echoed through the pantry, and it sounded like a..." She faltered. With an unsteady laugh, she added, "I don't know what it sounded like other than loud!"

As the volunteers returned to work, they continued to aim uneasy glances in Rachel's direction. As Isaac crossed the kitchen, Abby caught his eye. He guessed she was trying to pass some silent message to him, but he had no idea what it might be. If she was trying to urge him to be gentle with her friend, she didn't need to worry. He only wanted to make sure Rachel was okay.

"I'm fine," Rachel said before he could ask. "Please don't say anything. I'm embarrassed enough already."

Embarrassment wasn't the emotion glowing in her eyes, but he wasn't going to argue with her when so many ears were turned toward them.

"The girls must be much better," he said, though he wanted her to be honest with him about what had frightened her. "You wouldn't be here otherwise."

"They're fine and at day care."

"Waiting for choco puddin'?"

Her lustrous eyes grew wide. "Oh, *danki*, Isaac! In

the flurry to get us out the door this morning, I forgot to buy cocoa so I can make pudding tonight." Her smile became genuine. "The girls would have been heartbroken if I'd forgotten."

She was babbling. To divert him from asking the questions she wanted to avoid? Every instinct warned him something was amiss, but that he shouldn't push the issue. She had the right to keep her thoughts to herself.

Slipping past him, she carried the jug to where *kaffi* waited in a pot. She poured it in and closed the top.

"Gute mariye," murmured a silky voice from his other side.

Isaac turned and was surprised how he had to raise his eyes almost to a level gaze as he looked at a pretty blonde who stood right beside him. Her eyes were brown, and her lips were full and as red as fresh strawberries. He returned her greeting and introduced himself.

"Oh, you're Abby's big brother," said the blonde after telling him her name was Nina. "I've heard many *wunderhaar* things about you, Isaac." Her voice caressed his name. "I'm glad we've met at last."

"Me, too," he said, but his gaze cut toward where Rachel was packing cookies and muffins left over from breakfast into a plastic box.

"I'm sure we'll become *gut* friends." Nina's pleasant voice made him look at her. "Wouldn't you like that?"

He gave her a quick smile. "Excuse me. We need to get to work."

"See you later. Maybe we can get better acquainted during supper."

He went to where Rachel and another woman had finished packing the box with snacks for his team. The *Englisch* woman stepped aside so he could heft the well-filled box. His cousin Vernon came forward to get the jug holding the *kaffi*. They thanked the women for preparing the food for their midmorning break.

As he left with his cousin, Isaac turned to look over his shoulder. His gaze snagged on Rachel's and caught. Disquiet dimmed her eyes. He couldn't keep from wondering what had caused her to scream.

Isaac stepped outside. The rain had slowed to a drizzle, but the wind had picked up, so drops sliced into his face. He and Vernon walked with care on the slippery sidewalk.

When they reached the street running parallel to the brook, the few people they passed were aiming nervous glances at the water. He wanted to reassure them a rainy day wasn't going to recreate the disaster they'd suffered last autumn.

Isaac handed off the box to someone as he went into the house where the workers had begun hanging drywall. Soon the *kaffi* and the food were gone. The hard work made everyone hungry. After finishing his *kaffi*, he tossed the cup into a trash bag, then went to check the work in the larger bedroom. His team was skilled, but mistakes happened. Finding them before little errors became big problems was part of his job. He was pleased to see everything had been done right.

"She's pretty, isn't she?" asked Vernon as Isaac came back into the main room.

His cousin set a box of flooring on top of the others already stacked there. The boards would need a few days of sitting in the house and becoming accustomed to the humidity before they could be put into place. Otherwise, the boards would swell or shrink too much and leave gaps in the flooring.

"How many more boxes do we need to bring in?" he asked, ignoring the question.

"About a half dozen." Vernon leaned one hand against the low wall dividing the living room from the kitchen. "I answered your question, so why don't you answer mine?"

"You said someone was pretty. I didn't see a need to answer when I didn't know who you were talking about."

Vernon laughed. "You mean the pretty blonde or the pretty brunette? Some men would be grinning like a *dummkopf* to have two such lookers paying them attention."

"Nina was nice enough to introduce herself."

"Rachel was watching you every second of your conversation." He chuckled. "Except when you glanced in her direction. Guess she didn't want you to know she was keeping a close eye on you."

"You're being preposterous. Rachel was busy packing food for us."

"Me? Preposterous? What do you call yourself? I saw how you were looking at her. Not at the blonde, but at Rachel. Could it be, after all this time, you've found the woman for you?"

"All this time? You're older than I am, and you're still a bachelor."

"Maybe not much longer."

"Really?" He couldn't hide his surprise.

Vernon laughed. "*Ja.* There's this nice widow who's been helping with the painting over at the library, and she's a *gut* cook. Makes the best mincemeat pie I've ever had. A widow is used to having a man around, so I figure I won't have to change to meet her expectations."

"My step-*mamm* said something similar when she married *Daed*."

"Their marriage is what's made me think about the wisdom of courting a widow. Maybe you should think about it, too, cousin. Rachel Yoder is a widow with two little ones. I'm sure she'd be glad for a steady man in her life." He winked. "Besides, you know she's *gut* having *bopplin*. Her two are close in age, and you know how women are. As soon as one's out of diapers, they're pining for a new *boppli*."

Isaac wondered why his bachelor cousin considered himself an expert on women and *kinder*. On the other hand, there might be something to what Vernon said, but Isaac had learned long ago to make up his mind with facts he gathered himself.

The facts were simple. Rachel was a *gut mamm*, and she was an excellent cook and housekeeper. She wasn't bold with her speech or demeanor, and she never missed a church Sunday. She also kept her little girls entertained during the long service, a sure sign they'd been attending church since they were born. A hard worker, a *wunderbaar mamm*, devoted to God. Everything that would make her the perfect wife he'd been seeking.

Was God giving him a chance to see the perfect wife for him was here in Evergreen Corners?

Maybe, but he couldn't stop thinking of her extraordinary reaction to the commonplace sound of a cookie sheet striking the floor. Was there something she wasn't telling anyone?

He needed to find out.

Chapter Four

"I need someone to come with me," Abby called the next afternoon from the back door of the kitchen. "Anyone free?"

Several voices replied with an enthusiastic affirmative, including Rachel's. Getting out of the kitchen for a short time sounded like a *wunderbaar* idea. Nina had spent the day testing her patience and everyone else's, pushing the volunteers to their limits.

Rachel had never met another plain woman like Nina. She bragged like a sergeant Rachel had known whose platoon always won any challenge on the orienteering course. She'd grown accustomed to such bluster from him, because sergeants liked to rub others' noses in their victories. It was a way, she knew, to build camaraderie within a platoon, which was something invaluable when those men and women faced a real enemy. Even when the stories resembled superhero movies, it was part of the team-building spirit.

That wasn't the Amish way. Nobody boasted about their accomplishments or their family connections. Compliments were supposed to be met with a subdued reaction.

However, Nina hadn't been taught that. From the time she arrived in the kitchen—at the exact time to take a place front and center to serve breakfast after the rest of the volunteers had spent hours preparing the food—she'd listed the reasons why her family, her district and her community were the best.

Hailee and the other *Englischers* avoided Nina, because the blonde didn't seem to have any interest in impressing them. Her whole focus was on outshining the other plain women.

Rachel guessed it was because Nina was determined to find herself a husband in Evergreen Corners. Though she was surprised none of the men in Nina's home district had offered her marriage, she wondered if the blonde wanted to surpass her sisters, who were getting married.

Or maybe she was as unhappy at home as you were. The thought sent shame through Rachel. She shouldn't judge others when her own life and choices wouldn't have stood scrutiny.

However, her empathy for Nina didn't keep her from adding her voice to the others offering to help Abby with whatever she needed.

When Abby asked her to come grocery shopping, Rachel saw a few women looking relieved they hadn't been chosen. She understood. Wandering along the few aisles at Spezio's, the local supermarket, was often an exercise in frustration. The store wasn't set up to provide for a community kitchen, though the manager was eager to work with the relief groups.

They took the bus to the grocery store on the outskirts of the village. Right after the flood, the residents hadn't been able to get to the store without driving more than an hour each way.

Local people had become accustomed to plain folks in

their midst, so nobody paid attention as Abby and Rachel walked into the store. They each got a cart, and Abby pulled out two copies of her shopping list. Handing one to Rachel, she led the way toward the left side, where the fruit and vegetables were stacked in pleasing arrays.

"You find the things on the right half of the page, and I'll do the other side," Abby said.

Nodding, Rachel went first to the onions. She needed to get forty pounds, along with an equal amount of potatoes. Putting the bags in the cart, she had to smile. The bags weighed far less than either Loribeth or Eva, whom she hefted every day. Who'd have guessed toting around her *kinder* would provide a better workout than the two-mile runs she'd done daily in the Army?

"What's funny?" asked Abby as she set an armful of zucchini and squash in her cart. "You're grinning like a cat with a bowl of cream."

Rachel related her thoughts, leaving out the part about her military life. It was getting easier to navigate her way between the two worlds, but she mustn't get complacent. Doing that could ruin not only her hopes for the future, but also her girls'.

"I wonder if someone's written a self-help book on exercising with toddlers," she added as they reached the end of the aisle.

"It'd be a bestseller." Abby reached for a bottle of chili powder. "I appreciate your help today. My list was too long for me to bring the groceries home by myself."

"I appreciate helping."

Abby giggled. "I saw the look Nina aimed at you earlier."

"At me?"

"You know she doesn't like you, I assume."

It was Rachel's turn to laugh. "I think everyone knows Nina doesn't like me."

"Or anyone else."

"That's sad."

Abby's eyebrows rose. "I didn't expect you to say that."

"We've had a great time working in the kitchen. It's hard work, and it was *hot* work during the summer, but it's been fun." She took another container of baking powder off the shelf. "I learned a long time ago it's better to get along with people than be standoffish."

"Or proud."

"*Hochmut* should never be part of a plain life."

"That sounds like something someone said to you often."

Putting bottles of cinnamon and cumin into the shopping cart, she was glad to avoid her friend's gaze as she said, "Often enough."

She didn't want to think of her *daed* and how he'd snarled those words at her as he'd accused her of the sin of *hochmut* when she tried to explain she was innocent of whatever misdeed he'd believed she'd committed. He'd been furious she didn't dissolve into tears when he towered over her, threatening to hurt her more.

Defiance bubbled in her at the memories. She'd withstood what he'd handed out with his hand and his belt for as long as she'd been able.

Could he have been right? Was she proud she'd survived his abuse? She was, but that had to be different from the pride the ministers preached against. She'd survived by escaping, following the path God must have laid out for her, because she'd had no idea where she was going.

Abby pushed her cart forward a few feet, then stopped.

"I forgot garlic cloves, too. It's strange to get them from a store instead of the root cellar."

In spite of herself, Rachel flinched. The root cellar had been *Daed*'s favorite place to imprison her and her younger siblings. Years later, she had begun to wonder if he didn't want anyone to see the welts and bruises he'd caused. At the time, while locked in the dark, she could think of nothing but her pain and her fear, and her wish someone would let her out. Usually one of her siblings did after *Daed* had gone to bed, but once she'd been in the root cellar, forgotten, until *Mamm* came to get some vegetables for the next night's supper.

Mamm hadn't said a word, and Rachel guessed her *mamm* was terrified of *Daed* and embarrassed by how he treated their *kinder* and her inability to stop it.

"I wish Nina would be nicer to everyone," Abby said. "We've had such camaraderie in the kitchen. If you want my opinion, she's hiding some sort of hurt."

"I agree." She was relieved to speak of anything other than her past. "She makes such an effort to show she's superior to the rest of us, but I've found people who act that way often are the opposite. Or they think they are, so they do everything in their power to hide it instead of giving over their insecurities to God."

Abby moved the cart along the aisle to the next item on her list. "You sound as if you've encountered other folks like that."

"Enough to learn what's on the outside may not be the same as what's on the inside."

Rachel busied herself getting a dozen boxes of the pasta that was on sale, so she had an excuse not to say more. If she did, she might say too much. How sweet it'd be to tell Abby the truth!

By the time they reached the cash registers, their carts

were stacked so high Rachel kept a cautionary arm by hers. She guided it into the narrow space between two of the three checkout stands.

"It was much easier," Abby said as she began to put groceries on the conveyor to the register, "when Glen ordered the food and supplies we needed."

"Why did he stop?" Rachel asked as she put items threatening to topple from her cart on the belt, too.

"He's trying to bring the project to a close around Christmas. He's been spreading his duties among the rest of us. He handed off obtaining food to me." She pushed her empty cart forward so the young girl at the end of the checkout stand could put filled bags into it.

Rachel was relieved when, after paying, Abby had the store manager arrange for the heaviest groceries to be delivered by van to the community center. However, there were eight bags of perishable food to take with them.

The handles were cutting into Rachel's palms by the time they reached the bus stop. She was grateful when the bus rolled to a stop less than a minute after they arrived. When the doors swung open, the bus driver asked if they needed help, but before he could get up, two men offered assistance. Rachel handed over three of the bags and climbed onto the bus.

"*Danki*—thank you," Rachel said as she slid into the seat next to Abby and the men put the bags on the floor beside them. "You've been a *wunderbaar* blessing today."

The larger man blushed, and both men nodded before hurrying to take their seats as the bus moved onto the road.

Rachel leaned back. "Well, there's one big job done. Except for putting the groceries away. However, many hands should mean light work. Isn't that how the saying goes?"

"Sometimes you sound like Isaac."

"I'll take that as a compliment. Or is it? You complain sometimes he's too exacting in his comments."

"Isaac is exact with every aspect of his life, and I don't think you're any different. You like to have a plan for everything and a way to make the plan happen."

"If I give that appearance, I can assure you it's pretense. Most of the time since I've arrived in Evergreen Corners, I've been following orders. Do you think Isaac is like that, too?"

"My brother knows what he's doing."

"I didn't mean to suggest he didn't."

Abby grinned. "I know you didn't, but he's particular about being questioned about how he does things. I thought you should know."

"I'll keep that in mind, but I don't know if Loribeth will. She seems a little too pleased she threw up on his boots."

"He handled that better than I would have expected, but he needs to loosen up a little if he ever finds the perfect wife he's looking for and has *kinder* of his own."

An odd twist tightened Rachel's stomach, shocking her. Of course, Isaac would be searching for a perfect wife. He liked everything in his life to be in perfect order. That wife wouldn't be her…for more reasons than she could list. The most important was a former military officer was about as far from an ideal Amish wife as possible.

She managed to keep her voice light when she replied, "I should have guessed he'd be looking for a wife with you getting married. He won't have you to cook and keep his house."

"Does everyone in Vermont know I'm getting married?" She wagged a finger at Rachel. "We shouldn't be speaking of that until the announcement is published during a Sunday service."

"Maybe not everyone in Vermont, but anyone who sees you and David together can tell you're in love. Besides, friends always know these things, and I hope you count me as a friend."

"I do!"

Rachel laughed. "Don't you want to save those words for the wedding ceremony?"

Rolling her eyes, Abby chuckled. "Don't make me watch every word I say. I'll go crazy!"

"I would never do that." She'd spoken with too much fervor because her friend gave her a curious look. She wished she could explain she knew too well how it was to have to guard each word, but she silenced the thought. "So are you going to help your brother find a wife?"

"Me?" Her eyes widened with emoted horror. "Not me! Where would I find my brother the perfect wife he's looking for?"

"Is he serious? How could such a creature exist?"

"I asked him the same thing, but he seems to believe it's possible to find himself the perfect Amish wife."

Rachel laughed along with her friend, but she suspected Abby would jump in to assist her brother if she found a woman she thought would be a *gut* match for him. As much as Abby loved her brother, she would find matchmaking irresistible if she encountered a possible wife for him.

As long as Abby didn't consider Rachel a possible candidate. Trying to make such a match would prove to be a recipe for perfection all right. A recipe for the perfect disaster.

The bus came to a stop with the hiss of air brakes. Isaac paused on the sidewalk along with his future brother-in-law, David Riehl. They'd been checking the furnace being put into the last house the volunteers would be able to finish before winter. The ground began to freeze in late October, and they couldn't put in foundations after that.

Isaac appreciated David's skills with electricity and small motors. David had spotted a misplaced wire in the new furnace. It could be corrected before the unit was turned on.

When he saw Abby and Rachel stepping off the bus with bags of groceries, he called, "Could you use some help?"

His sister turned with a warm smile. When Rachel did the same, he was amazed to feel his heart give a peculiar beat he'd never experienced before. There was something about her expressions, open and honest, that made him want to find excuses to make her smile.

"We'd love some help." Abby held out her bags to David, who took more than half of what she held.

"Rachel?" Isaac asked.

"Danki." As always, she didn't say any more than necessary. Her smile had vanished, and she seemed fascinated with something on the sidewalk in front of her toes.

He lifted the bags out of her hands. He was surprised how heavy they were. Had she taken the weightiest ones for herself? He should have expected that, because she seemed to assume any task without complaint.

A hard-working woman is one of your criteria for a wife, said the small voice heard only in his head.

When the others began to walk toward the community center, Isaac followed. David continued to grin as Abby led their little parade. Isaac had come to see the man was, without question, the perfect match for his sister. They couldn't exchange vows until David completed his baptism classes and was more proficient in *Deitsch*. Plans were being made for the establishment of an Amish community in Evergreen Corners. Once that happened, church leaders had to be chosen. Any married man could become a part of the lot when ministers and a deacon were ordained. Isaac was certain his sister's future husband would be included among the possibilities once they were wed.

Rachel walked alone behind them, and Isaac increased the length of his strides to catch up with her.

"How are the girls feeling?" he asked.

"They're fine."

He'd hoped she would give him something other than the same clipped answers.

"I assume Abby's having the rest of the groceries delivered," he said.

"Ja."

His fingers tightened on the bags' handles. "Have I done something to offend you?"

"Offend me?" She stared at him with candid astonishment. "Of course not! Why would you think that?"

"Whenever I talk to you, you don't say anything more than you have to. I know you aren't curt with Abby, because she's told me things you've said that she's found insightful or amusing. So I'm wondering why it'd be easier for me to pull teeth from an angry bull than to pull words from you."

A flush climbed her cheeks, and he couldn't help but wonder if he'd made her more uncomfortable with him. "The truth is you intimidate me."

"I do?" It was his turn to be shocked. "I don't intend to."

"You don't need to apologize. It's just..." She paused and took a deep breath, then released it in a slow sigh. "I don't know what it is, but part is you're so important to the recovery effort, and I feel like I'm wasting your time."

"Nobody is any more important to our work here." The wrong tack, he realized when she edged away on the sidewalk. "Look, Rachel. Let's agree talking to each other without worrying about every word would be a *gut* thing. You and Abby are friends, and I can't think of any reason why we can't be, too. Can you?"

"No." When he thought she wouldn't say more, she added, "No, I can't think of any reason why we can't be friends, Isaac. It'd be easier for Abby if we were *friends*."

Had she put a slight emphasis on the last word, or was it only in his mind? He would have to change *her* mind that they could share more than friendship…if she continued to show how she could be the perfect wife for him.

Chapter Five

Lining up with the men to enter the community center, where they would worship together, Isaac glanced at where the women were doing the same. Rachel stood near the front of the line, one of the oldest of the volunteers, and he was the second eldest among the men. Only his cousin Vernon was older than he was.

The white-haired woman who was holding Loribeth's hand was Minerva Swartzentruber, the widow his cousin was walking out with. It was odd using such a youthful term to describe his cousin courting a woman who must be nearly sixty years old.

Wasn't he thinking of doing the same? Walking out with a woman who'd caught his eye? A woman who wasn't in her twenties any longer, either. He wasn't the same person he'd been when he was eighteen or nineteen and first considering it was time to look for a wife. Then, the idea of having another person to provide for had sent panic rising through him. He'd made their old farm in Lancaster County sustainable, but he'd spent every minute of every day working to keep people from knowing the truth about his *daed*'s craving for alcohol. Too many nights he'd wished he could have slept instead of tossing and turning with worry.

His life was his own. At last.

During the service while he sang, prayed and listened to the sermons from a pair of visiting ministers, Isaac prayed God would show him the best way to determine if Rachel was the woman he should ask to be his wife. His thoughts were interrupted when Eva crossed between the benches where the men sat facing the women. She climbed beside him and leaned her head against his arm.

She's fine, he mouthed when Rachel looked at him.

She gave him a grateful smile before bending her head to hush her older daughter, who was fidgeting beside her. Recalling how difficult it'd been for him when he was the little girls' ages to sit for the three hours of a Sunday service, he was glad to keep one of them distracted so Rachel could concentrate on the other.

He didn't have to do much distracting because two minutes later, Eva fell asleep. Soft breaths moved her tiny chest against the arm he curved around her to make sure she didn't fall. When they rose for a hymn, he shifted her off his legs. She murmured something but didn't wake until the service came to an end.

With a cheeky grin, Eva ran to her *mamm*. Isaac didn't follow, because Rachel would be joining the other women in serving the communal meal. Though they usually ate together every day, there was something special about the Sabbath luncheon, when the men gathered and spoke of the past week's work and the tasks awaiting them in the week to come.

Isaac wanted to linger, but went outdoors with the other men while the women and *kinder* ate. He waited for Rachel and her daughters to come outside, but he was called away by the mayor, who began by apologizing for intruding on his Sunday before she pelted him with questions about the current house projects. He was able to answer most of them, but had to call to other volunteers to provide information, taking them away from a game of cornhole, which was safer and easier to play on the village green than horseshoes.

During the conversation, Isaac kept glancing at the community center. Yet he missed seeing Rachel and her girls emerge, because by the time the mayor was reassured everything was going as scheduled, they'd already left. The men tossing the small containers filled with corn hadn't noticed where they'd gone. He asked everyone along the sidewalk, but they'd been too busy with their conversations to pay attention to anything else.

He'd have to go inside the community center. His feet balked. If he went in there and began asking questions about Rachel, he might as well wear a sign around his neck that he was interested in walking out with her.

As he stood, lost in the uncertainty of what he should do—a most peculiar sensation he couldn't recall feeling before—his sister emerged from the community center. A smile warmed her face when she saw him.

Without a greeting, she said, "Rachel is taking her little ones to look at the brook." Her eyes twinkled at him. "I thought you'd want to know."

"Did you?" he asked, not ready to admit he'd wanted to know. He'd wanted to know very much.

"*Ja*. You're looking for a wife, and as a *gut* sister, it's my job to point out when one is available for you to talk to her without a crowd around." She glanced past him. "Or you could wait until Nina Streit devises a reason to come over here."

He gave a cautious look in the same direction. The pretty, tall blonde he'd seen in the kitchen at the community center was surrounded by several lads too young for her. They were vying for her attention, and she was doling out smiles as if each one was the greatest reward on earth.

"I don't know much about her," Isaac said. "I suppose I should go and introduce myself to her."

"You've already been introduced to her. At the community center earlier in the week. Don't you remember?"

"Oh, *ja*," he said, though he didn't. If he did, he'd also have to admit that whenever Rachel was nearby, he found it difficult to notice any other woman.

"So what are you waiting for? Like I said, Rachel is heading to the brook." She gave him a gentle push. "She won't stay there forever."

Isaac settled his hat on his head as he took a meandering path toward the brook. It was a short walk there, and he heard the girls before he saw them among the few trees that had survived the flood.

Rachel had found a bank where the ground slanted gently toward the water. The closest houses were hidden by a thick row of tall, old-growth trees along the bank. Bugs chirped in the high grass, and more whirred in the air.

The little girls squatted until the front of their *schlupp schotzlis*, the white pinafores they wore over their best dresses, touched the clear bubbles caught between the stones. They were slapping the water with small sticks. When they were splattered, they giggled, their voices as sweet and high-pitched as the birds singing overhead. They all looked back as they heard the sound of his footsteps.

"Isaac!" Rachel exclaimed as he neared.

He understood the questions she hadn't asked but had been inferred in her surprised tone as she spoke his name.

What was he doing there? Why had he followed them to the brook?

Making sure his smile didn't waver, he said, "I'm sorry if I startled you."

"You did. I—"

Eva ran over to him. Holding up her branch, she said, "See, I-zak!"

"That's pretty," he said, not sure what she was trying to convey to him.

With a frown, she stamped her tiny foot. "Not pretty. Splash!"

"That's what I meant," he answered quickly. "It must make a pretty big splash."

Her smile returned, as if it'd never vanished. "Big splash!" She hopped to the edge of the brook.

As she teetered, he reached out to catch her. He wasn't quick enough because Rachel grabbed her first. He was left with his arms outstretched, facing Loribeth, who regarded him as if he was some disgusting thing she'd stepped into. The *kind* folded her arms over her chest and turned around. She couldn't have made her feelings about him any clearer if she'd shouted.

"Can we go?" asked Loribeth.

"Take off your shoes and socks," Rachel answered, "and give them to me." She picked up a crocheted bag he hadn't noticed on the ground. When the little girls obeyed and ran around barefoot, with Loribeth keeping a wide swath of ground between her and him, Rachel put the discarded clothing in the bag.

"Where are you going?" he asked.

"I saw some late blackberries across the brook, and we're going to pick some." She gave him a tentative smile as she pulled a small basin from the bag. "I hope the girls are still as enthusiastic about picking the berries after they get jabbed by a thorn."

"I never was happy to get stuck by a thorn when I was a kid! I don't think that will ever change."

"Me, either, but the berries are so sweet it's worth it." Her smile became warmer. "You're welcome to join us if you'd like."

"*Danki*. That sounds like fun, and I'm sure you can make something delicious with any berries we pick."

"You're welcome to take what you pick home."

"How?" He stuck his hands into the pockets of his church trousers. "Abby wouldn't be happy to find berry juice in my best pants."

She didn't laugh with him because Loribeth had jumped to a rock protruding from the water. The little girl teetered, then caught her balance.

"Wait for us," Rachel said.

Her older daughter began to pout, but giggled when foam from the water washed over her bare toes before she moved forward another stone.

Taking Eva by the hand, Rachel went to the shore to follow.

"Don't you want to take off your shoes and socks, too?" Isaac asked. "You're going to get them soaked."

Color washed from her face, and he wondered if she thought he was being too forward. He wouldn't have hesitated to say the same thing to one of his male friends, or to his sister, but everything he said or did around Rachel seemed to have shades of gray he hadn't considered.

"The water is low. I don't think I need to worry." She half turned. "Will you help Eva? I need to keep my brave Loribeth from tumbling into the water."

Had she noticed her older daughter's antipathy toward him? How could she not? Loribeth made no secret of it.

Holding out his hand to the littler girl, he asked, "Ready?"

She nodded, her eyes big with anticipation.

He said, "Let's go," then motioned for her to step onto the first flat stone.

The distance was too much for her short legs, so he grasped her other hand and swung her forward. She chuckled when her toes touched a stone.

Though he kept his eyes on Eva, he couldn't be unaware of Rachel a short distance in front of him. She'd convinced Loribeth to hold her hand, and they were skipping from stone to stone as if they were the same age. He paused, watching. He'd never seen Rachel so carefree before, and he had to wonder if this was how she'd been when her husband was alive.

It was odd how she seldom mentioned him. Was she as reticent with her girls? He tried to recall if he'd ever heard them speak of their *daed*. He thought of how Eva had rested her head against him during the church service, and a surge of sympathy filled him for Rachel's husband, who'd never had a chance to experience such a simple gesture.

As he swung Eva onto the opposite bank, she tugged her fingers out of his the moment her feet touched the grass, then ran after her sister.

Isaac stepped beside Rachel, who was watching them run, their arms outstretched as if about to take flight. "Looks like you didn't get your feet wet."

"I did." She shook one foot, and water trickled out of her sneaker. "It was either my foot or Loribeth in the brook. It's so hard to believe that sleepy brook did so much damage."

"I know, but look around and see the scars that haven't healed yet."

"Will Amish Helping Hands be able to get everything done by Christmas?"

He shrugged. "Guess we'll have to have everything buttoned-up by then. Not that we'll cut any corners. These people have suffered enough. They don't want a house falling down around their ears."

When Eva tumbled, a strident cry cut through the afternoon. Isaac rushed over and picked up the little girl, brushed dirt off her and reassured her she was okay. A moment later, she was chasing Loribeth.

He saw astonishment in Rachel's eyes. He realized his intrusion might not have been welcome.

"Sorry," he murmured. "I guess I spent so much time as a kid making sure Abby didn't get hurt, old habits kicked in."

"That's okay." She seemed as if she was about to add something more to him, then raised her voice and called, "Don't go so far!" She smiled as the girls paused, then kneeled to look at something close to the ground. "Loribeth would scurry to the ends of the earth if I took my eyes off her."

"And Eva would follow."

"*Ja.*"

"Let me give them a reason to stay closer." He bent and pulled out a wide strip of grass. Holding it to his mouth, he blew hard.

A sharp whistle rang through the air, and the girls' heads popped up. They ran to him.

"I-zak!" Eva exclaimed with a wide grin. "Again!"

"What did you do?" her older sister asked.

He opened his hand and showed them the blade of grass on his palm. "It's a grass whistle."

"Me, too!" Eva hopped around in her excitement.

He aimed a wink at Rachel. "You girls need to find

a blade of grass that's long and wide." He pulled on another long piece, loosening the sleek, green portion of new growth. "Like this."

Helping them find the proper-size blades, he saw their hands were filthy. Rachel wouldn't want them putting those dirty fingers to their mouths, so he led them to a spot where the bank was flat.

Rachel urged the girls to be careful as they splattered water in every direction. "You only need to rinse the grass, not agitate the water as if it's a washing machine."

"Shake it to get the water off it," he said and was rewarded with drops spraying over him as the girls swung the pieces over their heads. He raised his hand when Rachel was about to scold them. "I asked for it. I need to be careful what I say."

"They take everyone at their word. Their exact word."

"I get that." Motioning for the girls to come closer, he positioned his piece of grass with his thumbs on either side of it. "You need to hold it like this."

He waited until Rachel had helped the girls. Eva's thumb kept slipping until her *mamm* put her hands over her daughter's, keeping them in place.

Curiosity swept him. How would it feel to have Rachel's fingers against his work-hardened ones? Hers showed signs of years of working as well, but they weren't scarred and coarse like his. Hers cupped Eva's fingers as if they were as fragile and perfect as a soap bubble.

Isaac pushed the thought out of his head. Letting himself get caught in his imagination would be foolish. He couldn't become like his *daed* and lose himself in unreality.

"Hold the grass to your mouth and blow." He demonstrated, and another shrill whistle emerged.

The girls tried but couldn't make any sound other than their lips buzzing against their thumbs.

"It's a trick!" Loribeth scowled.

"Be nice," Rachel said. "It is a trick, but a *gut* one. It's one you can learn if you're patient, ain't so, Isaac?"

"*Ja.* Imagine there's a hole to one side of the piece of grass, and try to blow through it."

Eva looked from his hands to hers. Puffing out her already round cheeks, she blew hard. A faint sound emerged.

"Me did it!" Eva twirled in her excitement. "*Mamm*, me did it!"

"You did." She gave her daughter a quick squeeze.

Loribeth pouted. "Not me. I can't make it whistle. Stupid grass." She started to throw it aside, but Rachel halted her with a frown. "It won't work, *Mamm*. There must be something wrong with it."

"*Komm* here," Isaac said to the little girl. "Let me help you."

For a long moment, he thought Loribeth would refuse. Her determination to do everything her younger sister could do must have been stronger than her dislike for him because she edged closer. Not too close, he noted, and with enough space for her to make a quick getaway if he proved to be untrustworthy.

He shaped her hands around the blade. "Try it."

She did, but no sound came out.

"Blow hard," he urged. "Sometimes the grass needs to know who's the boss."

She drew in a deep breath that made her cheeks look like a chipmunk's, filled with acorns. Her face reddened as she blew. He heard a squeak before she whirled away from him and flung her arms around her *mamm*.

He watched while Rachel congratulated her daughter,

giving her a gentle hug. She clapped her hands in appreciation as the girls made silly sounds. She was a *wunderbaar mamm*. There was no doubt about how well she met the standards for his future wife.

Rachel was amazed how the afternoon had turned out. In her most absurd fantasies, she couldn't have envisioned Isaac playing with her girls and helping them pick berries. She tried to imagine their *daed* spending time with them, adjusting their hands so they could make a blade of grass whistle. She couldn't.

She wasn't being fair. Loribeth had been a *boppli* when Travis left for his last deployment, and Eva hadn't been born. Travis had been so excited both times she discovered she was pregnant. Though she knew he'd hoped for a son, he'd been thrilled with Loribeth. He would have been as happy, she had to believe, when Eva was born.

As she sat with her back against a tree, she wasn't surprised when Isaac dropped beside her. The girls could wear her out, and she was accustomed to their endless games.

"I'm not as young as I used to be," he said with a sigh. "Maybe I should have been like Eva and taken a nap during the sermon."

"I hope she wasn't a problem for you. She slipped away when I was trying to keep Loribeth quiet."

"She wasn't a problem. She was out like a light within seconds."

"She didn't sleep well last night."

"You'd never guess that to see her."

"Her nap gave her a second wind, it seems." Rachel smiled as she watched her daughters chasing each other through the grass. They paused to examine a leaf that intrigued them, then tossed it in the brook.

"Are your shoes dry?"

"Almost."

"I don't know how you can stand having your wet toes squishing around in your socks."

"It's no big deal. I get my feet wet almost every time I mop a floor." She forced a smile. "I've been called an enthusiastic mopper."

"You're the first person I've ever met who gets excited about cleaning a floor."

The conversation had taken an absurd turn, but she preferred that to explaining the true reason why she hadn't removed her socks. On her left calf, only inches below her knee, was a scattered pattern of scars. The medics had gotten her to the hospital after the improvised explosive device exploded. Nothing vital had been permanently injured, though they'd had to remove a few chips of bones along with the shrapnel. She'd been back to work within days, but the scars remained. Once healed, she'd forgotten about them until a neighbor in her new community asked about what had happened to her. She'd given some half answer about an accident while traveling, not mentioning she'd been in Afghanistan at the time.

Relieved when the *kinder* ran to join them, Rachel welcomed hugs from her girls. She tried to sort out what they were saying while they talked at the same time about the fun they'd been having.

"Me 'un-gy," Eva announced.

"Hungry," Rachel said when she saw Isaac's confusion.

"You 'un-gy, I-zak?" her daughter asked.

"Always," he answered with an easy grin.

Eva turned to her. "I-zak 'un-gy, too, *Mamm. Komm* eat? P'ease?"

Translating Eva's toddler words to mean she wanted

Isaac to join them for supper, Rachel wondered if he'd understood that, too. When she gave him a sideways glance, he was smiling at her daughter. Telling him she didn't have enough to share—which would be false—was something she couldn't do.

She hoped her voice didn't sound like fake merriment. "We've got macaroni salad and some cold leftover ham for supper. Would you like to join us?"

"Oh, *komm, komm,* I-zak," cried Eva, dancing about as if she stood on an anthill. "P'etty p'ease."

"How could I turn down an invitation like that?" he asked with a wink.

"Easy. Say 'no *danki,*'" muttered her older daughter.

"Loribeth!" Rachel chided. "What have Miss Gwen and I told you about being polite to others?"

"It's important." Her daughter's stance made it clear she didn't agree. "But Miss Gwen said—"

"There are no *buts.* I'm sure that's what Miss Gwen said."

"But, *Mamm*—"

"No *buts.*" Gentling her voice, she said, "Go and get your shoes and socks, please. Help Eva if she can't get her shoes on."

Loribeth stomped to where her shoes and socks had been left. Anger radiated from her.

"Are you sure it's okay for me to join you?" Isaac asked, his smile gone as his gaze followed her daughters.

"I wouldn't have asked if I didn't think it was okay."

"You may think it's okay, but I don't know if your older one shares your opinion."

"True, but she needs to learn to be nice to everyone."

"Not just people she likes?"

"That isn't what I meant." The familiar swath of heat that surrounded her whenever she said the wrong thing around Isaac—which she seemed to do with horrifying frequency—climbed up her face. "She got along fine with you when you were teaching them to whistle with grass."

"It was more of a truce than the beginning of a friendship."

"For Loribeth, that's a big deal." She sighed. "She wasn't happy when I first brought them here. Eva trusts everyone, but Loribeth's trust has to be earned."

"She dislikes change?"

"I'm not sure if it's that, though she's had plenty of changes in her short life. It may be the way she is."

"Like her *mamm*?"

Rachel's eyes widened, and she couldn't keep from staring at him. Was she as distrustful as Loribeth? She hadn't thought so, but it might appear that way to someone who didn't know how many secrets she was keeping.

"More like her *daed*, I'd say," she replied, knowing she must sound as if she didn't have any reason not to discuss this. "I see him in her."

"What about Eva?" Not giving her a chance to answer, he chuckled. "I'd say she's pretty much a miniature of you. She's warmhearted, and she isn't afraid of doing what she thinks is right."

"Oh, don't let her fool you. She can be more stubborn than her sister."

"Again like you, if I don't miss my guess."

"Well," she said, "we all have our faults, ain't so?"

She held her breath, hoping her words would be a reminder she wasn't the ideal wife Abby had told her he was seeking. If the circumstances had been different, she would have enjoyed spending more time with Isaac—with and without the *kinder*. But he was looking for a wife, and she wasn't ready to think about marriage, not until she was sure her girls would be happy with the choice she made.

"I don't see," Isaac said, "being stubborn as a fault. It means you're focused and persistent and know what you want out of life."

If only that could be true...

"Maybe I'll tell Miss Gwen that," she said, "the next time she says one of my girls is being as stubborn as an old mule."

"Who's Miss Gwen? You mentioned her before."

"She's the head teacher at the day care where the girls go while I'm helping in the kitchen."

"You must have made sacrifices to come to Evergreen Corners."

She wondered if he was curious how she could afford to be there. Few widows would have been able to leave their homes and volunteer their time, as she was doing. He had no idea she received a monthly military pension. She didn't use it for day-to-day expenses, but instead lived on the savings she'd accrued and on Travis's insurance. Her pension went to a bank account, waiting for the time when her daughters married.

"I've been glad to help," she said, "and it's been a *wunderbaar* experience for the girls to meet new friends."

"And you, too?"

She shouldn't look at him, but she did, and her gaze was captured by his dark brown eyes. Her answer to the question was important to him. Oh, how she wished she could come out and say he shouldn't consider her for a wife!

The perfect Amish wife, she corrected herself.

Somehow she needed to find a way to let him know she'd never be a perfect wife, most especially not a perfect Amish wife.

Chapter Six

The kitchen drain continued its steady *drip-drip-drip*. Rachel's attempts to tighten it by hand hadn't stopped the leak. She needed a wrench to put a halt to the puddles under the sink.

She pawed through the small toolbox that had been stored in the closet in her bedroom. Who kept a toolbox without an adjustable crescent wrench?

Sitting on her heels, she grimaced. So many times she'd reminded the men and women working in her transportation company to check their tools *before* they needed them. She could imagine the laughter if those soldiers ever discovered their company commander hadn't followed her own orders. She'd been foolish to assume her landlord had provided a complete set of basic tools.

Rachel set herself on her feet. One thing hadn't changed from her life in the Army. If she lacked something necessary to complete a job, she needed to find a way to get her hands on that tool.

She glanced at the clock on the stove. She was already late getting the girls from day care. She'd have to go to the store before she took them home. Glad she'd planned on leftovers for supper, she grabbed her bonnet and tied it under her chin as she hurried out into the warm afternoon.

Grateful that, for once, the girls didn't beg to linger a few extra minutes to play with their friends, Rachel walked with them to the store that wasn't far from the library.

It was tiny compared to the big-box stores on the edge of town, and she hoped somewhere in the muddle of merchandise there would be an adjustable wrench. She went to where tools were stacked in no particular order on the wall opposite the small post-office window. When she found what she was looking for, she tested the adjustments on the wrench. It should be perfect.

She was starting to show the girls what she was buying when Isaac came into the store. He noticed her, too, and he smiled as he walked toward them, as he had three days ago, when he'd joined her and the girls for a Sunday walk through the meadow on the far side of the brook. And just as it had that day, her heart began to dance within her.

Isaac grinned and replied to Eva's enthusiastic greeting. He glanced in Loribeth's direction, but didn't try to engage her in conversation. Though she had no idea why her older daughter had taken a dislike to Isaac, Rachel was relieved they seemed to have called a truce. At least for today.

Finally he looked at her, and her knees wobbled. She straightened them, determined to keep her heart from ruling her head, as had happened when she'd fallen for a man whose first love had always been his military career.

"Trouble?" Isaac asked in lieu of a hello.

She followed his gaze to the wrench she held. "We've got a drain that's leaking. I thought—"

"I'll check it if you'd like."

She halted herself from saying she was capable of

doing the repairs herself. Saying that could create questions. An Amish woman would depend on the men in her family to handle household repairs.

"Ja!" Eva shouted before Rachel could answer. "Make it stop, I-zak! P'ease, p'ease!" She began her impression of a dripping sink as she spun around him.

"I guess we'd appreciate your help," Rachel said as Isaac took the little girl by the hand. "Let me pay for this."

"I've got wrenches in my toolbox," he replied.

"I should have one at home. Just in case."

"Ja, you should, and I'll show you how to use it the right way." He smiled. "You're wise to be prepared for emergencies, Rachel."

"I don't know if a dripping sink is an emergency. It's just annoying."

"It's *gut* to be prepared for annoyances, too."

Rachel paid for the wrench with Loribeth close to her side. She noticed for the first time how her older daughter positioned herself to stand between Rachel and Isaac. Had Rachel betrayed her uneasiness about Isaac's interest in some way? She needed to ask Loribeth, but it would have to wait until after the sink was repaired.

Eva kept up a steady babble to Isaac as they climbed the sloping street toward the trailer. She talked about day care and her toys. Unsure how much Isaac understood, Rachel interjected an explanation here and there, where she could. Sometimes, *she* didn't comprehend what her younger daughter said.

As they passed the mailbox by the road, Isaac said, "Looks as if you've got mail."

She opened the half-ajar mailbox door. Pulling out flyers from local businesses, she saw an official-looking envelope. Her stomach dropped toward her toes. Even after she saw it was junk mail made to look important, her heart continued to thud against her ribs.

Travis's family had seen her decision to return to her Amish roots as an attempt to keep them from spending time with Loribeth and Eva. She'd assured them that she would bring the girls to visit as often as she could. In fact, while she'd lived in Maine, she'd sent letters offering to come to their home in Rhode Island. When she decided to go to Evergreen Corners to assist with the rebuilding and give herself a chance to recreate her life, she'd contacted them. That time their answer had been that, until she set aside her idea of becoming Amish, they wanted nothing to do with her. There had been a veiled suggestion her in-laws intended to consult with an attorney about getting the girls so they could raise them "as their father would have wanted," but nothing had come of it.

Not so far.

They hadn't responded to her subsequent letters. When she'd sent pictures of the girls as *bopplin*—pictures taken before she returned to the Amish—she hadn't received a reply. The situation broke her heart. The *kinder* had lost their *daed*, and she hadn't expected they'd lose their grandparents, too. They'd only known Travis's parents because she hadn't dared to try to sneak them to visit her *mamm*. The chance of encountering *Daed* was too great, and she didn't want him to ruin their lives as he'd attempted to ruin hers and her brother's and sister's.

In the kitchen, Isaac gave each of the girls a task to do so they could feel as if they were helping. Eva was sent to get old towels from the bathroom, and Loribeth was asked to hold a flashlight so it shone under the sink. Rachel was impressed anew about how well Isaac handled the *kinder*, even though it had been quite a while since he'd done the same with his brothers and sister.

He talked through every step he took to repair the drain. At his urging, Rachel leaned in as if she was hearing something new. Her daughters laughed when he explained how to know in which direction to turn the wrench. Rachel had to grab the flashlight from Loribeth as the two girls giggled and danced around the kitchen as they called out, "Righty tighty, lefty loosey."

"Want to try using the wrench, Rachel?" Isaac asked as he pushed himself out from under the sink.

"Sure." She squatted and held out her hand.

He placed it on her palm and explained how she should hold it to get the best torque. When she moved to reach under the sink, he put his hand on her elbow to steady it.

His touch had the opposite effect. Her usual firm grip on a tool wavered as her hand shook from the sensation of his work-roughened skin touching her.

"It's heavy," he said, his words brushing the fine hairs beneath her *kapp* at her nape. "Use two hands if you need to."

"No, I want to use it the right way. Learning the wrong way won't get anyone anywhere."

She heard his smile in his voice as he said, "True."

Giving the wrench a firm twist, she smiled, too, as the water oozing around the pipe stopped. "I think that's it."

He motioned her aside and checked the pipe. He set the wrench on the floor, then wiped moisture from the drain line. When no more drips appeared, he nodded. "Looks *gut*." Standing, he dried his hands on a towel. "It shouldn't *drip-drip-drip* now, girls." He bent to pick up the wrench.

Loribeth grabbed it. "Want to use the wrench."

"Me, too," Eva said, never wanting to be left out. Her lower lip protruded in a pout to match her sister's. "Use wench."

Trying not to laugh because releasing one emotion might undam the rest of them, and she needed to keep tight control while she stood close to Isaac, Rachel tapped her younger daughter's lower lip with her fingertip. "Leave this stuck out like this, and someone will put a teacup on it."

"No teacup!" asserted the little girl. "Want to use the wench."

"Wrench," Rachel said before she couldn't hold back her laughter any longer. "Wr-r-r-rench."

"That's what me said." Eva regarded her as if wondering whether her *mamm* had lost her mind. "Me want to use the wench."

"I think it's a lost battle," Isaac said with a chuckle. Leaning toward Eva, he asked, "Does your *mamm* have a toolbox?"

"Ja."

"Do you know where it is?"

Eva pointed to a spot in front of the stove. "Right there!"

"Can you two girls put this wrench into the box so your *mamm* can find it the next time she needs it?" He regarded them with a stern expression. "First, you need to get some cloths and make sure it's dry. Rusty tools don't help anyone. Do you think you can do that?"

Eva gave him an excited *ja*, and soon the two little girls were sitting on the floor with the wrench balanced between them as they dried every inch of it.

"Danki," Rachel said as she closed the door of the sink cabinet.

"That should keep them entertained for a while."

"Ja, but my *danki* was for your help in fixing the leak."

"I think your final twist did the trick." He gathered the damp towels. "You catch on quickly."

She kept her eyes lowered. Would they give away the truth she kept hidden? "I've got a *gut* teacher."

He beamed as she took the towels and carried them to the hamper in the bathroom.

Relieved he hadn't guessed he'd been teaching someone who was familiar with wrenches, she came into the kitchen to discover Eva had invited him to join them for supper. She hushed Isaac's protests that she didn't need to provide him with a meal, because tonight's supper might go a long way toward proving to him she'd never be viewed as the perfect Amish wife.

Isaac put away the toolbox and returned to the kitchen. He tried to find out if Rachel was okay with him staying for supper, but she brushed aside his words as she bustled around the small kitchen.

"Girls, get your cups and bring them to the table." She smiled over their heads as she added, "They're already learning to help."

"Training up a *kind* is important."

"It's easy when they want to assist me." She motioned for him to leave the kitchen. "And you can assist me by sitting and keeping the girls out from underfoot while I make our supper."

"You heard your *mamm*, girls. We're banished from the kitchen."

When Rachel suggested they color, her daughters collected books and crayons from a small box in the living room. They sprawled on their stomachs, and he had to take care making sure he didn't step on small toes or fingers as he edged out of the kitchen.

He bumped a rocker. Reaching out to slow its rocking, he ran his fingers along the simple carving on the thick wood. He wasn't a finish carpenter, but he could appreciate the artistry of an excellent woodworker.

"This is a well-made rocker," he said. "Where was it made?"

"Germany."

"Really?"

"Ja." She bent to stir the bowl of macaroni salad she'd pulled out of the refrigerator. She must be making sure the dressing reached the bottom of the dish. "I saw it in a catalog, and I realized how nice it'd be for rocking *bopplin* to sleep."

"So you had it brought from Germany?"

"Ja."

Was she extravagant with everything she set her heart upon?

"My husband," she went on, "saw how much I loved it and insisted we get it before Loribeth was born." A faint smile tipped her lips. "He said it was the least he could do when I was giving him a son to follow in his footsteps." Her smile broadened. "By the time Loribeth was born, the chair had been delivered, and we were happy to have a healthy daughter."

More questions pelted his mind, but Eva jumped to her feet and brought her coloring book for him to admire. She'd colored cows blue and the sky orange, and there was more color outside the lines than inside. She'd also added a few blobs of yellow that she informed him were the people looking at the cow: Eva, Loribeth, Rachel…and him. That he was included sent an unexpected warmth through him.

It stayed with him during the meal of ham, salad and potato chips. The girls had been delighted when he asked for chocolate milk, too. Loribeth thawed enough to tell him about how they'd found the chocolate milk at the store despite it being moved to a different location since their last visit.

When Rachel offered *kaffi* along with dessert, he accepted. The girls ate their apple pie and returned to their coloring on the floor before Rachel had a chance to set a cup and plate in front of him. He picked up his fork, eager to try the pie, which smelled so *wunderbaar*.

He cut through the crust and put a bite in his mouth. The spices exploded, thrilling his senses as he chewed. And chewed. And chewed. Even so, he had to swallow hard. He grabbed his cup and washed down the remainder with *kaffi*. He almost gagged because he'd forgotten to put sugar and milk into his cup.

"Are you okay?" she asked, and he realized she hadn't brought a piece of pie for herself.

"Of course. The pie is delicious. I don't know what special spices you put in it, but they're fabulous."

"You're being too generous." She poked at one of the crumbs on Eva's plate. "My husband used to say he liked my pie crust because it was resilient, like me. I know I'm not a *wunderbaar* pie-maker."

"Apple is my favorite pie, so I'm not fussy about anything but the filling."

"Is that a nice way of saying the crust is chewy?"

He searched for an answer that wouldn't insult her or her pie. "I'd say it's unique."

"*Danki* for your honesty. I'll never be the baker your sister is. Abby's crusts are so light she has to put filling in to keep them from floating away. I appreciate you being honest, as my husband was."

"Were you married for a long time?" he asked before he could halt himself.

"Six years almost to the day from when we said our vows to when he died after we found out Eva was on her way." She sighed. "I'm beginning to remember the *gut* anniversary more than the sad one."

"I'm glad. It's got to be better for the girls."

"I'm not sure it makes any difference to them. Loribeth may remember him, but I think it's more because of what I've told her rather than from her own memories. Eva never had a chance to know him."

"I didn't realize that."

"I try to talk about him to the girls, but sometimes it feels as if the time I had with him is melting away, inch by inch."

"Hasn't his family helped you keep his memory alive?"

"I don't hear from them often." She stood. "Would you like more *kaffi*?"

"If you don't mind." He would rather find out why her late husband's family seemed to have cut off her and the girls, but he recognized the resolve in her voice as she'd changed the subject.

The *kaffi*, once he added cream and sugar, was the best Isaac had had in a long time. Maybe his sister's pie crust was a bit more flaky—or a lot more flaky—but Rachel brewed a *wunderbaar* cup of *kaffi*.

Taking another appreciative sip, he gazed across the table and smiled at her. He was curious about her past, but her averted eyes had made it clear she didn't want to talk about it. He could respect that. Though they'd spent some time together during the past couple of weeks, they remained strangers.

He wished he knew a quick way to break through the barriers she kept in place. Grief must unfold in its own way. He'd learned that by observing his *daed*.

He continued to enjoy his *kaffi* as she put the girls to bed. When she returned, they spoke of the projects he was working on and the chances the work could be finished before year's end. He asked what her plans were when the aid agencies closed their doors in Evergreen Corners, and he wasn't surprised when she said she might remain in the small village. He could understand the appeal, because though he'd traveled often to his family's farm in northern Vermont, something had always drawn him back. Not only the work he could do, but also a community that connected plain folks and *Englischers*.

"I should get going," he said, noticing it was almost ten o'clock. In spite of his words, he didn't move. "*Danki* for the pie and the company."

"*Danki* for the lesson in how to use a wrench."

"Don't you mean 'wench'?" he asked as he stood.

When she rolled her eyes and shook her head, he laughed.

He was glad she was enjoying their conversation as much as he was. He hadn't wanted to leave while she was distressed.

Maybe it'd be better if they kept their conversations on the present, he decided as he bid her *gut nacht*. That would allow him to lead the subject to the future, specifically if they could have a future together.

Chapter Seven

In the clear warm light of morning, as Rachel worked in the community center's kitchen along with the other volunteers, it seemed as if the conversation she'd had with Isaac last night had been part of a dream. She tried to equate the laid-back man who'd faced her across her dining-room table with the person who always seemed focused on the next problem as he was dealing with the present one. She'd never expected the stern man who was obsessed with timetables sitting and enjoying cups of *kaffi* along with her pie.

She was grateful and disappointed he hadn't joined the volunteers at breakfast. Though she wasn't sure what she would have said to him, she would have liked to discover if last evening felt like a moment out of time for him, too.

Shaking her head, she tried to rid it of the cobweb of thoughts she shouldn't have been having. That everything seemed dreamlike could be explained by the gray morning and the downpour that had caught her unprepared after she'd dropped off Loribeth and Eva at day care. She'd been soaked before she could get back inside. With every step, her toes seemed awash in water inside her sneakers.

I don't know how you can stand having your wet toes squishing around in your socks.

She was shocked. The voice inside her head belonged to Isaac. It must have been because she was thinking about their conversation last night.

She was getting too involved with a man who was looking for something she wasn't. Getting comfortable with him could lead to her blurting out the truth. Hadn't she learned that last night, when she'd mentioned the rocking chair had been made in Germany? She'd stopped before telling him it'd been purchased while she was recovering in Germany after being wounded. At the time, Travis had seen it as a peace offering because he'd been insisting she resign her commission to be with their daughter. She'd asked him to become a civilian, too, but he'd resisted until his unit was deployed for what would be his final mission.

"Hey, Rachel! Are you awake over there?"

At Hailee's impatient voice, she wondered how long the young woman had been calling to her. She looked at the cleaning rag that had dripped on the table. How long had she been standing and thinking about things that couldn't and shouldn't be changed?

"Not quite," she called. "Need me for something?"

"Have you seen the big box we use for the midmorning coffee break? Abby can't find it."

"It's in the pantry. I'll get it."

"Thanks!" Whirling to do another chore, Hailee hummed a Clint Black song Rachel recalled from before she'd turned off the radio for the final time.

She went into the pantry and took down the large insulated bag, then carried it to where Abby had gathered food left from breakfast. "Here you go."

"*Danki*, Rachel," Isaac's sister said with a grateful

smile. Fatigue had left charcoal shadows beneath her eyes, and Rachel recalled that the youth group Abby oversaw with her fiancé was busy planning a hike before snow closed the mountain trails. "Can you pack muffins along with those chocolate-chip cookies?"

"Let me help," Hailee said.

They filled a box with treats. Rachel got some butter from the fridge and added a few plastic knives to the box. Zipping the top closed, she saw Abby stop on the other side of the table.

"You know how much I hate to ask this," Abby began with a wry smile.

"I know. It's my turn to take the midmorning snacks to the workers. Besides, I'm already wet." She wiggled her toes in her sneakers. "I make strange sounds when I walk."

Abby smiled. "At least take my umbrella."

"I'll be fine." She had no idea how she'd manage the box and the big container of fresh *kaffi* along with an umbrella. "Someone else can take the food for the afternoon break."

"Sounds like a plan." Abby patted her arm. "We appreciate your volunteering, especially today."

"Ja," interjected Nina as she paused by the table. "It wouldn't be right for one of us who's interested in finding a husband to be seen looking like…"

"A drowned rat?" Rachel asked as she hefted the box.

"Men like to believe a woman is always lovely, no matter the situation, and we shouldn't do anything to make them think otherwise." She looked at Rachel and sighed. "I guess you don't remember how it is for us younger women."

Instead of firing a sharp answer, as she suspected Nina wanted, Rachel put her hand against her lower back and leaned forward as if gripping a cane. "You're right. We old folks don't understand you young whippersnappers."

Laughter came from around the kitchen, and Nina's eyes narrowed with unspoken anger. She flounced away as Rachel straightened.

"Be careful," Hailee warned. "She could be a dangerous enemy."

"Only if we want the same thing, which we don't." She felt a prickle of guilt, but she couldn't consider a future with Isaac when he wanted a perfect wife. Not that Nina would be a perfect Amish wife, either, but at least she didn't have a past as a military officer and she could give him the family Rachel could not.

Abby handed her the thermos. "She thinks her smiles will reduce men to blithering idiots eager to do her bidding."

"From what I've seen, she may be right." Rachel shifted the two containers so she wouldn't drop either.

"A blithering idiot isn't what I was looking for in a husband."

"Maybe Nina is."

"Do you think it would cause too much of a scandal if I told her to go home?" A wistful note filled Abby's voice.

"You're assuming if you asked she'd listen to your request."

"True." Abby smiled. "*Danki*, Rachel. You always put everything in the proper perspective. I'm sorry it's your turn to go to the building site today."

She started to shrug, then thought better of it as the insulated box shifted. She carried the food out to the main room, then put it down long enough to pull on her wet coat and soaked bonnet. She picked up the boxes and thanked Hailee, who helped by tossing Rachel's cloak over her and what she carried.

Rachel went out into the storm. She was certain it'd be easier to walk with the bulky containers than with her daughters, who were always tempted to run and look at something that intrigued them, no matter what the weather.

The village appeared deserted except for a few people who'd gathered on the bridge over the brook. They looked upriver toward the ruined covered bridge and then downstream. She'd seen a handful of residents go onto the main bridge with every storm. A bank of dark clouds above the mountains to the west drew more people to the bridge. She nodded as she walked past them, but didn't stop to ask what they thought they might be able to do if the brook rose to a dangerous level, as it had last fall. They wouldn't be able to stop the wild waters, but she guessed they didn't want to be taken by surprise again.

The buildings were being repaired and the roads repaved. Bridges had been reconstructed, and trees had been replanted. However, it'd be far longer before anyone who'd lived through the flood would have peace of mind.

The building sites weren't far from the covered bridge. One set of wooden arches had been stripped of everything but a few deck boards. Atop the other set, the bridge seemed to tilt more with each passing day. Would it collapse into the brook before it could be repaired? She knew the mayor was fighting red tape to get funds, but so far the state hadn't considered the bridge a priority, because there were alternate ways to get to the homes on either side of the brook.

If her transportation unit had been there, they could have put down a roadbed and erected a temporary structure to protect the antique timbers in no time.

Rachel might as well wish the flood had never happened. She hurried through the strengthening wind to where three partially built houses were set side by side overlooking the brook. The road separated the house sites from the brook. In the hurricane, water had swept the original houses off their foundations. From what she'd heard, furniture from only one of the houses had ever been found, and that had been downstream near a lake. Everything from the other two houses had vanished.

The ground around the building sites had been trampled bare. Grass and weeds tangled beyond the areas where the volunteers worked. Nobody was outside on the rainy day. The two houses without roofs stood deserted, so she guessed everyone was inside the one that offered some shelter.

Going inside, she heard several workers call, "Shut the door!"

She smiled as she shook rain off her bonnet. The warning sounded as if it'd been said enough times to become singsong. With the house weatherproofed, the volunteers were determined to avoid the elements they'd worked in during the past months.

She couldn't blame them. She was grateful every day for the cooler weather, so it was possible to catch one's breath in the community center's kitchen.

"Coffee's here!" shouted a woman dressed in bib overalls and a bright red shirt. She was, if Rachel recalled correctly, a teacher at the elementary school.

Every head turned, and Rachel's eyes were caught by Isaac's. He stood on a board straddling two sawhorses while he worked near the ceiling. She was astonished to see he was wiring a ceiling fan in place, but knew she shouldn't be. Though Amish didn't have electricity in their homes, they did in their barns and businesses.

He jumped down, then took the *kaffi* container and set it on the board where he'd been standing. She put the box of muffins and cookies next to it. She grabbed the box when it wobbled.

"It's okay," he said, chuckling as he handed her a towel to wipe her soaked hands and face. "The sawhorses aren't the same height."

"Are you sure it's not an uneven floor?" she asked, surprised to hear herself teasing him within earshot of the other volunteers.

A tall plain man she knew was named Michael Miller rolled his eyes like an irritated teenager. "You wouldn't joke about such things if you had any idea how many measurements Isaac insisted we take before we set the first joist."

"And for the second and third," added another man from the other side of the room.

More grumbles laced with laughter came from every direction around her.

"See what you've started by questioning the quality of our work?" asked Isaac.

Rachel joined in with the laughter, and the bad taste left by Nina's snide comments vanished. "I'll know better from now on."

"Do you want to see what we've done?"

"*Ja*, once I pour the *kaffi*."

He motioned to one of the men. "Jose will be glad to do that so he makes sure he gets a full cup today."

The man who wore a cheerful grin said, "I didn't complain much about having only a half cup yesterday."

When several of the volunteers snorted their disagreements, everyone chuckled.

Isaac took the cup held out to him and snagged a pair of cookies before motioning for her to follow him. After taking off her shawl, coat and bonnet so she didn't track water through the new house, she peeked through doorways into rooms set off by two-by-fours. Wiring ran between the studs. Hand tools were placed close to the walls, but she had to slalom around the larger equipment.

"It's beginning to look like a real house," she said as he finished the second cookie. "How much longer do you think it'll take?"

"About four to six weeks. Once the drywall is up, we'll put on joint compound. That needs to dry before we can begin painting. We'll install the cabinets and fixtures. Floors go in after that. At the same time, the exterior will be painted. That will finish the project, and we'll move on to our next-to-the-last house." He gave her a wry smile. "You can see why I'm concerned about finishing by year's end. I think we'll have to divide the team to get both houses done on time."

"I'm sure you'll figure it out."

"Without cutting corners."

"You're going to have to cut some corners off boards."

His mouth quirked. "You know what I meant."

"I did, but it's fun to pull your leg. The girls don't get my sometimes absurd sense of humor."

"Or they're wise enough to ignore your words." Not giving her a chance to retort, he asked, "How are the girls doing?"

His simple question opened the door to the memories of last evening, and she found herself tongue-tied, as she'd been the day he'd helped her take the *kinder* to the *doktor*'s office. "Okay."

"Not making their regular mischief?" He looked at his work boots. "If one shines more than the other, it's because it got a *gut* cleaning after Loribeth threw up on it."

She despised the heat rising along her face. "I should have said this before. *Danki*, Isaac, for being a big help since the day the girls got sick. I should have—"

He halted her by putting his finger against her lips. Shocked by the spark that raced from his skin to hers, she could only stare at him.

Swallowing hard, he drew back his hand. "You've thanked me too much already, Rachel."

He grinned, but the easy expression didn't reach his hooded eyes. What was he trying to hide? That he'd felt something unexpected when he touched her, or he'd noticed her reaction and realized he'd made a mistake?

She wondered how two siblings could be so different. Abby couldn't hide a single thing she felt because it was displayed on her face. Isaac was the definition of a closed book, concealing what he thought behind correct words. Wasn't she doing the same? Last night in the trailer, she'd veiled her thoughts behind an offer of a cup of *kaffi* and a taut smile.

She must respect his secrets if she didn't want him to probe into hers. She must make sure he never suspected she was anything other than the widow he saw in front of his eyes.

Isaac drove a nail into a board, swinging the hammer with the power of his frustration. What a *dummkopf* he was! What had he been thinking? He shouldn't have given in to his yearning to discover if Rachel's lips were as soft as they looked. Not when they were in a house filled with other volunteers. If they'd been seen...

He grabbed another nail and banged the hammer on it, grazing his thumb. Startled, he stared at the reddened digit. He hadn't hit himself with a hammer since he'd been a boy. That had been his first lesson. Keep his eye— and mind—on what he was doing while using tools.

He'd been thinking about Rachel and how her bright blue eyes had widened when his fingertip touched her mouth. She looked away, but not quickly enough because he'd seen more than shock in her gaze. He'd seen a softening there, an invitation he wasn't sure she intended to offer him.

"Having trouble keeping your mind on your work?" asked his cousin Vernon as he brought an assembled light to go onto the fan Isaac had been hanging when Rachel arrived.

"Trying to figure out how we're going to get everything done in time," he said.

"In the house or with something else?" Vernon laughed, then added in a near whisper so nobody else could hear, "So I see you've decided to court a widow, too. Or were my eyes—and everyone else's—deceiving us?"

"I'm not going to dignify that stupid question with an answer." Isaac pulled a tape measure from his belt. "We need to get to work."

His cousin continued to chuckle as he went on to his next task. The older man wore a knowing grin every time Isaac spoke with him that morning. The rest of the crew was more circumspect, but Isaac couldn't help overhearing whispers when he walked past.

When it was time to stop for the day, he was relieved. Today, it'd seemed everyone was more interested in gossiping than working. Why couldn't others mind their own business? The question had plagued him while he tried to keep the neighbors from learning about his *daed*'s alcoholism. He didn't want to deal with it again.

Isaac was fighting a headache by the time he dragged his grim mood up the steps to the garage apartment. He was tired of the sideways glances, tired of whispered speculation, tired of the rain and tired of worrying about the schedule that seemed impossible to meet.

He was met by the aroma of beef stew as he entered the apartment. His sister had changed her work schedule so she cooked meals at home two nights a week, but she often left something on the stove for him and went to David's house to eat with him and his daughter.

Abby came out of the kitchen, wiping her hands on her apron. She smiled. "Did you have a *gut* day, Isaac? Rachel said you're making great progress on the house. She enjoyed the tour you gave her."

"Not you, too, Abby," he grumbled as he placed his hat on the peg by the door with more fervor than necessary. It careened off, and he had to retrieve it and slip it on the peg.

"Not me, too? What are you talking about?"

"Vernon has been bugging me since Rachel brought food for our break this morning. Maybe you should send someone else with the *kaffi*."

She folded her arms in front of her. "I could send Nina or Hailee, I suppose, but I'd have to explain to Rachel you don't want her there."

"No, that won't work."

"The first part or the second?"

He rubbed his brow. His headache was strengthening and threatened to crack open his skull. "Can't we talk about something else? Let's eat." He took a single step toward the kitchen and gasped when his knees buckled beneath him.

Abby leaped forward and caught him, steering him toward the sofa in one smooth motion. When he collapsed on it, she placed a hand against his forehead.

"You've got a fever, Isaac. I think you've caught the bug that's going around."

"Don't be silly! I've got too much work to be sick."

"As if germs ever check our schedules."

He groaned, unsure if the sound was from the abrupt pain in his gut, or the thought of how many on his team could sicken if he'd passed the bug on to them. They already were cutting it close in their race to finish the houses before the aid agencies shut.

Then he'd have to go home to the family's farm up north. Could he return to the life he'd left behind, a life of secrets and half truths? Could he leave without letting Rachel know he believed she'd be the perfect wife for him?

Chapter Eight

"Look who's back among the living!" someone shouted from the community center's main room.

Laughter reverberated into the kitchen.

Rachel hurried to the pass-through window and was pleased to see Isaac, though gray under his eyes, looked otherwise fine. When she'd learned he was sick, she'd wanted to help, but Abby, while grateful, had been determined to keep Rachel and her daughters from being exposed to Isaac's germs.

She watched as his crew welcomed him as if he'd been gone for two years instead of two days. He grinned at their teasing, but his gaze swept the room. When it struck hers, she gripped the edge of the pass-through and didn't look away. He'd become so much a part of her life during the past couple of weeks that it'd seemed as if a strange void had been opened when he didn't stop by to play with Eva and try—yet again—to persuade Loribeth they could be friends, too.

She missed him.

Plain and simple. Missed him as she hadn't missed anyone since Travis went away on his final deployment.

Would it be as painful when Isaac left Evergreen Corners at year's end? She tried to tell herself his going would be for the best.

But as their gazes connected and locked, she wondered how much longer she could pretend she'd be satisfied with being his friend and nothing more.

Isaac crossed the room toward her, and she stepped out of the kitchen. The other voices in the room became muffled as she said, *"Gute mariye."*

"Gute mariye."

"How are you feeling?"

"As someone said, I'm among the living," he said with a smile that made her fight to catch her breath. "It wasn't the same bug the *kinder* had, though it had similar symptoms. So you don't have to feel guilty that I caught it from your girls."

"I wasn't. They were sick too long ago."

"So why are you on edge?"

She didn't want to tell him how worried she'd been—how worried she *was* about him leaving Evergreen Corners in a few months—but she also refused to lie. "No more than you are, Isaac Kauffman, when I'm sure you spent your recovery time worrying that even a single sick day will keep you from finishing those last three houses before the end of the year."

"Abby shouldn't have said—"

"Abby didn't say anything. I know you and how you've been fretting about the projects."

He squared his shoulders. "A man doesn't fret, Rachel."

"What would you call being concerned about every detail of every project, how it'll be done and when, how much it'll cost and what will happen if everything isn't finished to your standards by the end of the year?"

"Dedication."

She laughed, glad he felt well enough to jest. "Call it whatever you want. It's fretting."

"She's right," Abby said as she joined them. Giving her brother a quick hug, she grinned. "You were worse than ever when you weren't feeling *gut*."

Looking from his sister to her, Isaac said, "I hope she didn't tell you I threw up on her shoes."

Rachel's eyes widened. "You did? How awful for…" She wasn't sure if she should feel sorrier for Isaac or Abby.

"He's joking, Rachel," Abby said as she wagged a warning finger at her brother, who burst into laughter. "He kept everything down fine."

Firing a frown in his direction, Rachel said, "It's not like you to tell a lie, Isaac Kauffman."

"I didn't tell a lie." He struggled to speak past his guffaws. "I said I hoped Abby didn't tell you I threw up on her shoes. Guess I didn't add I hoped she hadn't because it wasn't true."

"See what I have to endure?" his sister asked with a martyr's sigh. "Nobody realizes how he pokes fun at people he's close to."

As brother and sister continued to debate in *gut* humor, Rachel wished she could hold Abby's words inside her heart. Isaac teased people he was close to? That must mean he was feeling close to her. She allowed herself to savor the idea a moment before pushing it aside. Isaac wasn't looking for a friend, she reminded herself. He was looking for a perfect Amish wife to give him a perfect Amish family and a perfect Amish home.

Abby was called away with a question, and Rachel started to follow. She paused when Isaac spoke her name.

"Rachel, I need to ask you a favor." He reminded her

of Loribeth when she was unsure if she could get away with something naughty.

Naughty? Isaac? The two words didn't go together. Though she'd discovered other sides to him than the strict martinet she first had believed he was, he walked a very straight path.

"What can I do to help?" she asked.

"I've got an appointment in half an hour to look at a farm that's for sale at the edge of the village."

"You're thinking of buying a farm here?"

"Just looking. I'd appreciate it if you'd give me your opinion."

"Of a farm? I've never run a farm."

"You've lived on one. More important, you've lived and worked in a farmhouse, and I'd like your insight into the house. Is it something that would work for me?"

She translated his question to mean he wondered if the house would become a *gut* home for him and his wife and family. "I'll be glad to look at the house for you. It's the least I can do after all you've done for us."

His eyebrows lowered. "I don't want you to feel you've got to say *ja*. You aren't beholden to me for anything."

"You've helped—"

"You've helped, too. Keeping score isn't what we're supposed to do. God expects us to offer our hands and our talents to others without obligation."

She lowered her eyes from his frown. "*Es dutt mir leed*, Isaac."

"You don't have anything to be sorry for, so don't apologize. I thought we were friends, and friends do things for each other without keeping track." He paused, then raised his chin and asked, "Rachel Yoder, without either of us fulfilling or creating an obligation of any kind, would you visit the house this morning and give me your honest opinion?"

At the humor in his voice, she looked at him. Even a week ago, she wouldn't have believed anyone who told her Isaac's eyes could twinkle that brightly.

"Ja." She intended to add more, but halted when Nina pushed between her and Isaac.

The taller woman didn't glance in her direction. "Isaac, how lovely to see you!" She wore one of her scintillating smiles as she put a bold hand on his arm. "Did I hear you say you're looking for opinions about a house you want to buy?"

For a moment, Rachel was envious of how comfortable the blonde acted around men. She pushed aside that thought as soon as it formed.

From the kitchen doorway, Abby mouthed *I'm sorry*, but Rachel wasn't sure if the words were for her or Isaac. Nina was already talking as if she was going to make a home on the farm with Isaac. Nina batted her eyelashes at Isaac as she linked her arm through his and steered him toward the door. For a moment, Rachel hesitated. Maybe she should take this as God's way of reminding her she shouldn't stand in the way of what Isaac was seeking.

Then he turned and shot a desperate glance in her direction. Rachel didn't need Abby's murmured urging to follow the two out of the community center and into the cool, crisp morning. As she tied her bonnet under her chin, she caught up with them along the sloping sidewalk. She ignored the pointed scowl Nina aimed in her direction and fell into step with them. Isaac glanced at her and winked, his expression growing serious when he turned to Nina.

Rachel knew he was glad she'd come along, and she was glad, too.

* * *

When the real-estate agent, a pleasant middle-aged lady, dropped them off on the dirt road that curled along a hillside above the brook, Rachel wasn't surprised. Ahead of them was supposed to be the farm lane. It had become a field of brambles like the briars enveloping Sleeping Beauty's castle. As long as a fiery dragon didn't hide in their depths… A plain woman shouldn't be thinking about dragons in briar patches or the firepower needed to root out the creature.

Beside her, Nina sniffed with disgust. "Someone needs to cut the brush around here. How do they expect anyone to see the house when it's surrounded by a jungle?"

"The previous owner died," Isaac said as he led the way into the bushes, hacking them with a large knife the real-estate agent had given him before she returned to her car. When he looked at the house, which was half-hidden by trees, he sighed. "His heirs are elderly, too, and that's why they're selling the place."

"It's sad," Rachel interjected into the strained silence left by Isaac's words, "when a farm can't be kept in a family that's been the one to husband the land for so many years."

"It is." He glanced over his shoulder as he added, "Be careful your clothes don't get snagged on the thorns."

Nina made a despairing sound, and Rachel was surprised when the younger woman continued to follow them instead of turning back to the road. In spite of her efforts, Rachel had to unhook her apron twice from prickles, and the second time jabbed her finger. She stuck it in her mouth for a moment as if she was no older than Eva, then continued to push her way through the snarled greenery.

She gave a sigh of relief that echoed Isaac's as she

emerged from the briar patch. Waiting for Nina to escape the tangle, she noticed leaves stuck to his suspenders and scratches on his arms.

"I didn't realize," he said in an apologetic tone as the blonde emerged, "how we'd have to hack our way in. If I had, I would have cleared a path before I invited anyone else here. I'll make sure the path is wider before we leave."

"That's so kind of you, Isaac." Nina brushed leaf debris off her light blue dress and regarded him with wide eyes. "You're always thoughtful of others."

"What do you think of the place?" he asked, looking at Rachel.

She appraised the scene before them. Rusty red and muted gold mums needed to be trimmed near the porch. A beautiful sugar maple was a mixture of orange and green, as the leaves began to don their autumn colors. Lilac bushes had grown too close to the house and concealed windows. A section of gutter along the roof was sprouting tiny trees where seeds had taken root in the debris that had collected and rotted there. The small leaves offered the only color because weather had stripped off any paint. Gray clapboards were beginning to curl at the edges.

"I think," she said, "there's potential here. It must have been beautiful once. With the underbrush cut and flowers blooming throughout the summer, it'll look *wunderbaar.*"

"I'm glad you can see that." He smiled, but turned as Nina pointed out the tilting weathervane on the main barn.

Following them toward the house, Rachel was glad the porch steps were intact. Nodding when Isaac handed her a key and suggested she and Nina go inside while he went into the cellar to check the furnace and foundation, Rachel hurried across the porch's creaking boards.

The front-door lock was reluctant to move, but she leaned her shoulder into it as she twisted the key and turned the knob. The door opened with a squeak that grated on her ears.

She walked into the kitchen with Nina on her heels. The house smelled of mildew and neglect. Dust clung to every surface, including cobwebs woven into the corners of the windows. Dead bugs were strewn across any flat surface, and the walls were dim with grime.

However, the kitchen cabinets were maple and not sagging. The large woodstove was from an earlier era, but when she opened one of the doors, she was pleased to see there was no rust inside. Elbow grease and cleanser would have it shining in no time. She couldn't say the same for the nearby range. It was so filthy she couldn't be sure what its original color had been.

A table in the center of the floor had seating for eight. Several more chairs were arranged along the walls wherever there was enough space. She could envision a large family eating at the table, along with the hired men who would have helped in the fields and with the milking a few generations ago.

"It stinks in here," Nina began, then paused as the door opened and Isaac walked in. "However, any *gut* Amish woman could have this cleaned in no time."

Rachel thought Nina was being overoptimistic. Hours and hours of work would be required to get the house into livable shape. Spiderwebs were weighted with dust, and her feet stuck to the floor with every step. She imagined getting a power washer to take the top layers of grease and burned-on food off the stove. She didn't want to think what that oven must look like, and she intended to avoid opening the refrigerator door. She guessed it was filled with mold and other things she didn't want to come face-to-face with.

Isaac gave the kitchen a cursory glance, then walked into the living room beyond it. She explored the first floor with him and Nina, who was struggling to maintain her sunny attitude.

When Isaac wanted to check out the barns, Rachel returned to the kitchen. She opened a door that led to what had been a laundry space. The washer rusting in silence was older than she was by several decades.

Nina waited in the middle of the kitchen, her arms clasped in front of her.

"I can't imagine anyone living in this disaster."

Closing the laundry-room door, Rachel motioned toward the table. "It was a family home at one time."

"Whoever did the cooking for that many people must have spent her whole life in the kitchen."

"Let's hope some chairs belonged to daughters who helped put three meals on that table every day."

"Until they found someone to marry." Turning toward Rachel, she mused, "Speaking of marriage, can I give you a word of advice?"

"If you feel you need to."

Nina didn't take the hint in Rachel's cool answer. "If you think being sentimental is the way to that man's heart, you're wrong."

"Really?"

"*Ja.* Anyone should be able to see Isaac Kauffman is a practical man. Men like him don't like mushy comments about flowers." She gave Rachel a satisfied look from beneath her lowered lashes. "I'm surprised you don't know that. You've been married."

"My husband used to bring me flowers." She didn't

add that the bouquet was almost always an attempt at an apology after he'd been delayed and come home late from hanging out with his men after practice maneuvers.

Nina waved away her words. "What worked with him won't work with Isaac, so if you think you can persuade him to walk out with you, you—"

"I don't have any plans to marry Isaac."

"No? I heard you talking about husbands."

"What? When?"

"When we were stuck in those briars."

Rachel searched her memory, then laughed. It was the wrong reaction, she realized, when Nina's expression became stormy. For a moment, she considered letting the young woman stew in her misunderstanding, but that wouldn't be what God would expect of her. She needed to be honest.

"I was talking about husband," Rachel said, "in the way that a family husbands a piece of land, bringing forth its bounty."

"I knew that," Nina said in a superior tone, though her eyes suggested the opposite, "but I wanted *you* to be prepared if Isaac misunderstood you."

"*Danki* for pointing that out."

"My pleasure."

Rachel saw no reason to continue the conversation, so she headed for the stairs to the second floor. The blonde didn't follow.

After peeking into four filthy bedrooms and a disgusting bathroom, Rachel opened another door. Stairs led up to the attic. They were dotted with half-chewed acorns and dead bugs, but she climbed, her curiosity stronger than her distaste. She peered over the top of the stairs. Boxes and chests were pushed up to one side, and the floor was covered with more than an inch of dust. She started to step onto it, but paused when she heard her name called.

Looking down, she saw Isaac with Nina close beside him. Would he be upset that she was exploring what could become his home? If so, she saw no clue of it on his face as she returned to the second floor.

"Anything up there?" he asked.

"Some stuff in storage." She wiped the hem of her skirt. "And lots of dust. How were the barns?"

"Like the house, they need work. I've seen enough for this visit. Have you seen enough of the house?"

"Enough to know it needs a *gut* work frolic." As they walked down to the living room, Rachel ran her hand along the banister that had been smoothed by many fingers before hers. "It'd be great fun to discover what's stored in the closets and in the chests under the eaves."

Nina wrinkled her nose, but Rachel wasn't sure if it was in disagreement, or she'd caught another of the odors that didn't seem to bother the blonde as much when Isaac was in the house.

"I'm sure it's nothing but junk," Nina stated. "As far as *practical* matters go, the living room is a fair size, but you'll have to take a wall down if you plan to hold church Sunday services here."

"We're few in number."

"The community will grow. At least, I know you're hoping it will." Her eyelashes fluttered.

Rachel pretended to cough so she could hide her annoyance with Nina's blatant flirting. Isaac turned to her with exaggerated concern, and she saw he was having a tough time concealing his amusement at Nina's attempts to beguile him.

When Isaac suggested they take a more roundabout route to the road, Rachel nodded along with Nina. They walked out into a field that, unlike the briar patch around the farm lane, had been cut earlier in the summer. Rachel watched where she stepped because it became obvious a herd of cows had been there not too long ago. She realized she should have mentioned that fact when Nina gave a sudden screech and waved her foot in the air. Her face was so distorted with disgust and outrage, Rachel couldn't hold back a laugh.

"It isn't funny!" Nina cried. "I stepped in cow manure."

"Wipe your shoe on clean grass and be grateful you weren't barefoot," Rachel said.

"It wasn't cow manure," Isaac added. "You stepped in a mud puddle, Nina. Rachel's right. Just wipe your shoe on the grass."

Annoyed, the blonde stamped away in the direction of the road.

Rachel put her hands over her mouth, but couldn't silence her laughter. Nina had looked like Loribeth when her nose was out of joint. It wasn't kind of Rachel to react that way, and she'd have to apologize to Nina later.

She looked at Isaac as a rumbling laugh burst from him. It was *wunderbaar* to share a joke with him, more *wunderbaar* than it should have been. She'd worry later about their relationship, which was becoming too complicated. For now, she gave in to laughter.

Rachel's laugh, Isaac decided, was perfect. Filled with music and glee and honesty. Once she released it, he doubted it could ever be recaptured because it wafted like a robin's song on gentle breeze.

It was a sound he was sure he'd never grow tired of.

"Oh," she murmured, "that wasn't nice of me."

"Of us," he amended with a grin.

"You wouldn't have laughed if I hadn't." She rolled her eyes as she added, "Nina won't make it easy for me to say I'm sorry."

"She will if you assure her that you won't ever tell anyone that she thought some wet mud was cow manure. No Amish woman on the husband hunt would want her potential mate to discover she knows nothing about cows."

"Are you always so deviously clever, Isaac?"

"If I said you inspire me, would that be an acceptable answer?"

When she began to walk in the direction of the road, he matched her steps. She smiled as she said, "That would make me the devious one then, ain't so?"

"Would it?" He chuckled, amazed how easy it was to be himself around Rachel. She didn't expect him to take the lead every time, and when she asked a question, he knew she wouldn't take his answer as the final word. She had a quick and practical mind that he found intriguing.

"I don't know." She glanced at the buildings behind them. "What will you do next?"

"Run some numbers for repair costs. There's no milk tank, so everything will have to be kept in pails until I can get a tank put in."

"Is there electricity for the tank?"

"*Ja*, but I'd want to upgrade it. If I do decide to buy this farm, I'll want to put in a refrigerated tank so I can sell my milk as Grade A."

"There are a lot of cheesemakers in Vermont, and they're fine with Grade B milk. You might want to do other improvements first. You can move to Grade A milk after you've gotten in your first harvest and you're familiar with your herd and what they're capable of producing."

He looked at her with astonishment as they left the

field and crossed through the narrow strip of trees toward the road. She had a rare gift for getting to the crux of a problem and presenting a solution he might have overlooked. If she'd been born a man, he guessed she would have been running a successful business.

As they stepped onto the narrow, twisting road, he said, "That's a *gut* point, Rachel, though I'd have to haul around milk pails. I've got lots to consider. Most important, my family lives hours north of here."

"Abby plans to stay in Evergreen Corners after she gets married."

"True." He couldn't add how he continued to worry that his *daed* would lapse into his dependence on liquor if Herman couldn't make a success of the farm in the Northeast Kingdom. "First, I'm going to have to run the numbers to see if it's feasible."

"And pray for God's guidance."

"That goes without saying." But he was glad she'd said that. It showed her faith was strong and as much a part of her as breathing.

Had a potent faith been one of the criteria for the woman he hoped to marry? It must have been.

While he was weighing the pros and cons of purchasing the farm, he needed to do something else, too—figure out how to persuade Rachel that she'd be the perfect wife for him.

Chapter Nine

Isaac sat in the community center the following week and listened to the rain pouring from the eaves. The volunteers had finished their meals, and only Abby and a few other women remained. They were cleaning up from supper and making preparations for tomorrow's breakfast.

So he waited for his sister, who'd forgotten to bring an umbrella with her. He'd offered to go to their garage apartment and retrieve it, but she'd said they wouldn't be much longer and asked him to wait.

That had been over an hour ago.

He looked at the page in front of him. Columns of numbers had been crossed out or erased. He was trying to calculate the cost of getting the old farm into *gut* enough shape that he could make some money to reinvest in it.

The list of what needed to be done was longer than he'd guessed when he paid his first visit to the farm. A second trip with the real-estate agent three days later had shown him even more work that had been delayed almost too long. The roof on the main barn rested on rafters that were beginning to bow. The door to the hayloft hung by a single hinge. The concrete in the milking area had begun to crack and chip, a danger to any cows that didn't watch where they were going. Or for a man hefting heavy milk cans and carrying them into the storage area.

That was just the main barn. The equipment shed needed its right wall shored up, and what he guessed had been a chicken coop wasn't salvageable. Its future would be as kindling for the stove.

He rubbed his forehead and sighed. The house needed as much attention as the outbuildings. Was he insane? He'd become accustomed to having a crew of skilled carpenters when he worked on the new houses. At the farm, he'd have to work alone until he earned enough money to hire help.

Maybe Rachel was right about selling Grade B milk to begin with, that small voice in his mind counseled.

Rachel…

He was no closer to introducing the idea of marriage into their conversations. Each time he'd seen her since their first trip to the farm, she'd been with her daughters. Talking about the future while she had toddlers in tow seemed ridiculous. He recalled how Abby had talked a couple of days ago about David taking her out for *kaffi* and pie at the village diner again. They'd gone there when they first started working with the teen group, and she said it was a *gut* place to talk.

A smile unfurled on his lips. Was Abby matchmaking again? His sister hadn't mentioned anything about him walking out with her friend, but maybe she'd decided to resort to more subtle methods.

"Oh, Isaac, I hoped that was you!"

At Nina's voice, he folded the pages and shoved them into his pocket. She'd already asked too many questions about when he was going to move onto the farm, and he didn't want to be rude and tell her he was trying to decide *if* he wanted to purchase the property.

"Do you need something, Nina?" he asked.

"Abby mentioned you had an umbrella."

"Ja."

"I don't have one here." She gave a faint shudder as she glanced at the front door. "It's raining hard, ain't so?"

"Ja. Would you like to borrow my umbrella?"

"Then you and Abby would be left without one." She widened her eyes. "Would it be too much trouble for you to walk me home?"

"Of course not." He stood, expecting her to back up a few steps. She didn't, and he found his face uncomfortably close to hers. Edging away from her burgeoning smile, he said, "Go and get your things while I tell Abby I'll be right back."

Something flickered in her eyes, and her smile wavered. He didn't wait to hear what she had to say. Instead, he strode into the kitchen. It seemed deserted other than his sister, who was mixing dough for the muffins the women would bake in the morning.

After he'd told her his plans, Abby dropped her spoon into the bowl with a clank that sounded extra loud in the quiet space. She regarded him with an unusual frown that straightened her lips. Her voice wasn't more than a whisper. He guessed she didn't want it to carry past his ears. "I don't know why you let her rope you into taking her home."

"She doesn't want to get soaked."

"Is that what she told you?"

Isaac scowled at his sister, wondering why she was making such a big deal out of doing a fellow volunteer a favor. "Why are you asking silly questions?"

"I asked one question, and it wasn't silly. I know you're

"One Minute" Survey

You get up to **FOUR** books <u>and</u> Mystery Gifts...

YOU pick your books –
WE pay for everything.
You get up to FOUR new books and TWO Mystery Gifts
absolutely FREE!
Total retail value: Over $20!

Dear Reader,

Your opinions are important to us. So if you'll participate in our fast and free "One Minute" Survey, **YOU** can pick up to four wonderful books that **WE** pay for!

As a leading publisher of women's fiction, we'd love to hear from you. That's why we promise to reward you for completing our survey.

IMPORTANT: Please complete the survey and return it. We'll send your Free Books and Free Mystery Gifts right away. **And we pay for shipping and handling too!** *We pay for EVERYTHING!*

Try **Love Inspired® Romance Larger-Print** books and fall in love with inspirational romances that take you on an uplifting journey of faith, forgiveness and hope.

Try **Love Inspired® Suspense Larger-Print** books where courage and optimism unite in stories of faith and love in the face of danger.

Or TRY BOTH!

Thank you again for participating in our "One Minute" Survey. It really takes just a minute (or less) to complete the survey… and your free books and gifts will be well worth it!

Sincerely,

Pam Powers

Pam Powers
for Reader Service

"One Minute" Survey

GET YOUR FREE BOOKS AND FREE GIFTS!

✓ Complete this Survey   ✓ Return this survey

▶ DETACH AND MAIL CARD TODAY! ▶

1 Do you try to find time to read every day?
☐ YES   ☐ NO

2 Do you prefer books which reflect Christian values?
☐ YES   ☐ NO

3 Do you enjoy having books delivered to your home?
☐ YES   ☐ NO

4 Do you find a Larger Print size easier on your eyes?
☐ YES   ☐ NO

YES! I have completed the above "One Minute" Survey. Please send me my Free Books and Free Mystery Gifts (worth over $20 retail). I understand that I am under no obligation to buy anything, as explained on the back of this card.

☐ I prefer Love Inspired®
Romance Larger Print
122/322 IDL GNTG

☐ I prefer Love Inspired®
Suspense Larger Print
107/307 IDL GNTG

☐ I prefer BOTH
122/322 & 107/307
IDL GNTS

FIRST NAME

LAST NAME

ADDRESS

APT.#

CITY

STATE/PROV.

ZIP/POSTAL CODE

LI/SLI-520-OM20

interested in finding yourself the perfect wife, but you can't be thinking Nina is the one you're looking for."

He was astonished his sister would speak of matters normally shrouded in secrecy. Even siblings were sometimes surprised when plans to marry were published by a couple they hadn't realized were walking out together. She might drop hints he should walk out with Rachel, but she'd never asked him if he was.

She must have taken his silence as a reprimand because she squared her shoulders and looked him straight in the eye. "Well, don't say that I didn't warn you." She strode away, vexation coming off her like a wave of heat.

He sighed. Nobody would ever describe his sister as tight-lipped or accuse her of hiding her opinions. Everyone knew what Abby Kauffman was feeling and thinking.

Years ago, he'd been the same, but that had changed when the family responsibilities fell on him. He hadn't wanted the community's disapproval to focus on his *daed*, who hid his alcoholism well most days with Isaac's help. If the deacon or the bishop had learned of the problem, they would have come to confront his *daed*. The eyes of the *Leit* would have been upon the whole family, and Isaac hadn't wanted his siblings to bear the humiliation of the truth being shared throughout the district.

After walking out of the kitchen, he put on his hat, found his umbrella and opened it and the door. Nina slipped her hand onto his arm and pressed up against him as they went out into the rainy evening. Too close for his comfort, but he didn't say anything as they crossed the wet grass of the village green. She pointed out the house where she was staying. It had a broad porch, which allowed them to get out of the rain.

"Danki," she murmured as he lowered the umbrella

and gave it a gentle shake. "Would you like to come in, Isaac?"

"I need to take Abby home."

She smiled at him. "You could do that and come back. I made some cookies we can share. They're delicious."

"*Danki*, but I'll say *gut nacht*."

Her eyes snapped with abrupt anger, and he half expected her to stamp her foot as Loribeth might have. At the thought of the *kind*, Rachel's pretty face filled his mind as his sister's words rang through his head.

Abby was right. Nina Streit wasn't the woman who could make him the perfect wife. Rachel was, and he needed to find out if she would be willing to marry him. He'd put it off for too long while he fiddled around with calculations on the funds needed to close on the farm and make it productive. The numbers on the farm were clearcut, and so was his decision about Rachel.

That was why after leaving Nina on the porch and returning to the community center, he hurried his sister home so quickly she struggled to keep up with his longer strides. He threw open the door at the top of the stairs and motioned for her to go inside. When she did, he remained on the landing.

"Are you going somewhere?" Abby asked in a tone that suggested she already knew the answer.

"For a walk."

"In the rain?"

"I've got some things to think about, and walking always helps me think."

As she began to close the door, she looked around the edge and grinned. "Say hi to Rachel for me!" Her laughter remained after she'd shut the door.

Isaac gave in to a wry grin. He should have known he couldn't fool his sister. Abby had been hinting—and more than hinting—that he didn't have much time to waste in thinking about asking Rachel to walk out with him. He was aware of how little time they had remaining. It was nearly October, and the work in Evergreen Corners was scheduled to be done around Christmas.

He and Rachel weren't youngsters any longer. There weren't singings and other youth-group events for them to ride home from together. She had *kinder* to consider. If it'd been summer, he might have arranged for a van to take them to Canobie Lake Park in New Hampshire. He'd enjoyed trips to Hersheypark amusement park as a youth and had heard fun stories about Canobie. It was too late in the year for that.

By the time he'd walked to Rachel's home, he'd talked himself in and out of a half-dozen ideas. He'd still made no firm decision when he knocked on the door.

It opened, and the *kinder* stood there. Loribeth regarded him with open distrust, but Eva grinned at him. He couldn't keep from smiling back. Rachel's daughters were adorable…like their *mamm*.

A screech came from beyond the girls. Both whirled and squealed with excitement.

"Kitty!" called Eva and raced away.

When Loribeth followed, for once trailing behind her little sister, he stood on the front step, unsure if he should go in or not.

"Shut the door!" Rachel shouted.

He lowered the umbrella, stepped inside and closed the door in a single swift motion. The *kinder* spun about and ran toward him, chasing something small. It ran into his boots, caromed away and stared with unblinking eyes.

A tiny kitten.

It sped around him. The girls gave chase. Backed into

a corner by the kitchen cupboards, it turned, arched its back and hissed.

Rachel came into the room, her hair loosening from beneath her *kapp*. There was something endearing about her dishevelment, and she resembled her daughters more than ever. "Isaac! I didn't realize—" She jumped aside as the kitten and *kinder* raced toward her.

"Where did you get a wild cat?" he asked, trying not to laugh. "And why?"

Instead of answering, Rachel rushed after the kitten. She'd almost captured the little beast twice before. Each time, the kitten had eluded her, skittering away as she reached for the tiny ball of fur. Cornering the tiny cat, she edged closer, then jerked back her hands before they could be scratched—again!—or bitten—again! She watched the four-ounce, long-haired calico fiend race past her and into the girls' room. Her daughters followed, giggling with delight.

"That is Sweetie Pie," she said as she looked at her hands, which were striped with bloody scratches. "Most cats have five claws on each foot. That misnamed creature has seven toes on each of her front ones, and I'm going to have the scars to prove it."

"I didn't know you were planning to get a cat." Isaac set his umbrella against the wall and put his hat on the peg beside her bonnet.

"Neither did I. The girls think she's cute and sweet, which is why they've named her Sweetie Pie. I think she's planning to murder us in our sleep tonight."

When he took her by the arm and led her to the sink, he turned on the faucet and cleaned her scratches.

"Ouch!" she said as the water hit a deep one.

"Sorry." Sympathy filled his eyes, which were far

more expressive than Rachel would have guessed they ever could have been when she'd first met him.

"It's okay," she said, though it wasn't. The incisions left by the kitten's claws burned as if she was holding a match to them. "You wouldn't want a maniacal kitten by any chance, would you?"

"Not likely." He glanced at the *kinder*, who were using a string to tempt the cat to bat at it. "I think you'd have a mutiny on your hands if you get rid of their latest pet project."

She groaned, not from pain but from his silly pun. "I know, but a kitten is the last thing I needed."

"So why did you get one?"

"A parent came to the day care today with a box of kittens." She opened a tube of antibacterial ointment. "I was able to talk the girls out of bringing home two, but they refused to leave without one they can share."

"Diabolical of those parents."

"Without question." She dabbed more ointment on the bleeding scratches. Wincing, she said, "I thought they'd enjoy having something to take care of and love. However, as the saying goes, no *gut* deed—"

"Goes unpunished." He gave her a crooked smile. "What are you going to do with the kitten when you have to be at the community center?"

"She's litter-box trained, or so I've been assured. I plan to put her in the bathroom with her box and some food and water until she becomes tame enough not to rip the whole house apart." She smiled and shook her head. "After that, the cat and the house are in God's hands. I hope He leaves both intact."

"I'll add my prayers." He stepped aside as Eva ran into the kitchen after the cat. "You're going to need them."

Rachel watched in amazement when Isaac bent as the

kitten and *kind* raced past him. He seized the kitten by the scruff. Her odd paws wiggled as if she was trying to run through the air, then she calmed as he continued to hold her suspended as her *mamm* would have. Waiting while her breathing slowed, he began to pet her. He spoke nonsense words to her as she grew calmer, her eyes blinking as she struggled not to give in to sleep.

"That's incredible," she breathed as Eva stared wide-eyed at the kitten that was still for the first time since they'd brought her home.

Loribeth paused at the far end of the kitchen, her gaze focused on Isaac, but she didn't move any closer.

"It comes from years of chasing kittens in the barn. You learn when to grab them and how," he said. "Do you have a bed for her?"

"Ja," Eva said. "She no like."

"Really?" he asked, squatting in front of the little girl.

Eva reached out a tentative finger and ran it along the kitten. The faint buzz of a purr startled the little girl.

"That means she likes you," Rachel assured her.

"By growling?" asked Loribeth as she inched closer.

"It's not growling. It's a sound kitties make when they're happy."

With a wide grin, Eva said, "She like Eva."

"She does."

"I wasn't sure she could purr at such a young age," Rachel said.

"I read somewhere," he replied, "that young bobcats purr."

"That makes sense, because she's as wild as a bobcat."

Isaac looked at Eva. "Where does Sweetie Pie sleep?"

"With me?" Eva asked, her eyes wide with hope.

"Not tonight. Tonight she's going to sleep in the bathroom." Rachel motioned for them to follow her.

As she passed her older daughter, she caught Loribeth's hand and smiled. Her daughter remained somber, and Rachel gave a silent sigh. She wished she had some idea why Loribeth disliked Isaac. Her attempts to find out had caused her daughter to end the conversation by picking an argument with her sister.

When Loribeth tugged away, Rachel asked, "Don't you want to tuck Sweetie Pie into bed?"

Her daughter looked from the kitten to Isaac, torn.

He must have seen her reaction, because he said, "Let me put Sweetie Pie in her bed, and I'll get out of the way while you say '*gut nacht*' to her."

Rachel put her hand on his arm in a silent *danki* as he slid past her in the narrow hallway. He glanced at her, and the powerful emotions in his eyes nearly staggered her. For the briefest second, before he turned away, she'd seen the truth. He continued to consider her a possibility for his wife.

As her heart reeled with delight, she wanted to shout he was about to make a huge mistake. He didn't even know her real married name, a name she'd never used in the Army, so it'd been easy to set it aside when she decided to return to her Amish roots.

You don't know the real me, she wanted to shout after him. *If you did, you'd walk out the door and never return.*

She shuddered at the thought of Isaac shutting her out of his life, but went with her girls into the bathroom as soon as he'd retreated toward the kitchen. Her daughters sat on either side of the box they'd lined with several towels to make a nest for the kitten.

While Rachel whispered to the girls, the kitten gave a soft hiss, but her heart wasn't in it as she surrendered to sleep. Loribeth put a doll's blanket on the kitten. Instead of growling at her and striking out, the kitten nestled into the towels, curled into a ball with her tail pointed at her nose.

Her daughters were reluctant to go to bed, but did when she reminded them Sweetie Pie would be up early in the morning. After chasing the kitten and her litter-mates throughout the day, Loribeth and Eva were asleep, too, almost before Rachel turned on their night-lights and closed their bedroom door.

She leaned against it for a moment, trying to steady her breath as she thought of going into the living room, where Isaac was waiting for her. He'd come over in the rain. Why? He wasn't there to ask her to marry him to-night, was he?

Rachel squared her shoulders and walked away from the door. All she could do was pray their friendship could be salvaged. She had to believe that was possible, or she would do something foolish.

Like agree to be his wife when she was the wrong woman for him...

Chapter Ten

Raking leaves was backbreaking work, and Rachel's muscles were threatening to explode from a dull ache into searing pain at any minute. She wasn't accustomed to such physical work, and she hadn't guessed what a chore it'd be to get leaves off the grass. There were only two trees in the front yard, but every tree along the street, and most in the woods behind the trailer, had donated to the collection on her lawn. She suspected she could have called her landlord, and he would have sent someone over to get rid of the leaves. She couldn't, not when he was letting her and the girls stay there while she served with Amish Helping Hands. She must not repay his kindness with demands for a job she could do herself.

The trash-removal company was coming soon to take away any leaves raked to the street, and she wanted as many gone as possible. She hated doing lawn work. It was, she knew, another remnant of her childhood, when mowing the grass and raking the leaves and shoveling the snow had been her tasks. While other young girls had gathered for frolics and had the chance to spend time with young men from nearby districts, she'd had to stay at home and do her chores.

With a laugh, she said aloud, "You know there's a story about that, Cinderella."

"Cinderella?" asked Eva, her ears attuned to anything any adult said, as always. "What Cinderella?"

"Not a what, but a who. Cinderella is a girl who needs to do her chores to help her family, and she never complains." She smiled. Sometimes it was difficult to recall how she hadn't known much about fairy tales when she was a *kind*. Most she'd discovered after she'd jumped the fence and had to read them in order to understand references made in her new *Englisch* life.

Doubt crept into her mind. Were her in-laws right? Was she denying Loribeth and Eva a part of their heritage? As they grew, she planned to share more about Travis and the *Englisch* life they'd lived before his death. It was impossible to live in two such different worlds, and trying to do so would confuse her daughters. They were at an age when they were willing to accept what she offered them. Would they always be that way? She couldn't keep from wondering if, when they were older, they'd decide to jump the fence, as she had. Would they come to resent her, and tell her that she'd deprived them of the life they would have had if Travis hadn't been killed? Or would they come to treasure a plain life, as she did?

Shaking aside the uneasy thoughts, she paused and watched the girls chasing Sweetie Pie around the yard. There were years ahead of them before Loribeth and Eva had to make the decision of how to spend the rest of their lives. What mattered was that they knew she loved them, no matter what they chose.

She smiled when Eva slid on a small patch of leaves and tumbled to the ground, then jumped to her feet to run after her older sister and Sweetie Pie. Though the kitten had snarled and swiped her paws at Rachel for the first two days she lived with them, the connection between the tiny creature and her daughters had been instantaneous.

When Sweetie Pie rushed to where Rachel stood, the kitten leaned against her leg for a short second before scurrying away. Her smile broadened. That was unexpected. For some reason she couldn't fathom, the kitten had had a change of heart this morning and didn't hiss and scratch each time Rachel got near. Maybe Sweetie Pie had decided if she wanted to be with the *kinder* who doted on her, she had to be nice to their *mamm*.

Or maybe the kitten had figured out which member of the family kept her food bowl full.

"Look at you!" called Abby as she crossed the leaf-speckled lawn, carrying two grocery bags. "Out enjoying a beautiful fall day."

"*Enjoying* may not be the right word." Rachel gave her back a rub. "No, it's not the right word."

"I know Isaac would be glad to help."

Not being honest with her friend about Isaac's visit a couple of nights ago was troublesome, though there really wasn't anything to tell Abby. As soon as she'd gotten the girls settled for the night, the kitten had begun to mew loudly, protesting being left alone. That had upset her daughters, and she'd been glad for Isaac's help in calming the kitten while she convinced the *kinder* to go back to bed. He'd left soon after that, as if he'd been concerned that she'd blame him for the kitten's noise. She'd been sorry he'd headed out so quickly, but she had been relieved at the same time.

She almost told Abby that, but didn't. She couldn't explain her fear that Isaac might propose and that she might listen to her heart.

Her silly heart, which seemed to believe there was a

way for her to give it to him and find happiness together despite her past.

Her misguided heart that had already persuaded her to marry Travis when she'd known his career was more important to him than any wife and family could ever have been.

She would be a *dummkopf* to listen to it again.

She couldn't say that. Instead, she shook her head. "Isaac has enough to do already. He wants to have those new houses..." She paused. "What's the word he used?"

"Buttoned-up." Abby set her bags on the trailer's front steps. "Don't let his worrying get to you. He laments every evening how much work needs doing before the houses are weatherproof. He must say 'buttoned-up' at least a dozen times every evening. Do you have another rake around here?"

"No, you're not going to help, either. You've been working every day for the past two weeks at the community center, as well as making supper for your brother and for David and Mikayla."

Abby's smile softened, as it did when anyone mentioned the man she planned to marry and his daughter. "It's an excuse to see more of them."

Rachel leaned her rake against a tree and came to sit beside her friend on the steps. She opened the container next to them, then filled four glasses with bright red juice. She gave two to her daughters and then offered the third to Abby.

"Don't ask what flavor it is or how much real juice is in it," she said. "The girls love it, so I know it's got lots of sugar in it."

"No kidding," Abby replied after taking a sip. "It might be all sugar."

"But it's wet, and that's what I need." She tilted her

cup and drained it. "If you drink it fast, you don't have to taste it as much."

They laughed together, but neither reached to refill their cups.

"The girls are having fun with their new kitten," Abby said. "They're going to exhaust the poor little thing."

"Or she's going to exhaust them." She smiled. "Either way, they should sleep well tonight. It's *gut* for them to have something to take care of."

"You sound like Isaac. He's always saying we need to be responsible for ourselves and those around us." Her friend's easy expression fell away. "I shouldn't joke about it. If it hadn't been for Isaac, I don't know what would have happened to our family after *Mamm* died. My *daed* had…a problem." She glanced at Rachel. "He had a problem with alcohol. He never was fall-down drunk, but when he drank, he drank to excess."

"I'm sorry." She was, because she knew how difficult it was to live with a parent who was a disappointment.

"It's better now since *Daed* remarried, but Isaac carried the weight of the farm and raising us during the years when he should have been a carefree teen whose only thoughts were of getting a courting buggy so he could convince some cute girl to let him take her home."

"I had no idea."

"Of course you didn't. He never talks about things from the past." Her eyes narrowed. "Like you don't. You've both buried your pasts and don't let anyone help you."

She didn't have a quick answer for that, because it was the truth, so she shouted to her girls to come closer to the house. "If that kitten goes in the street, I'm afraid they'll follow."

Abby hesitated, and Rachel guessed her friend wanted

to return to what they'd been discussing. However, when Abby spoke, it was about the coming week at the community center and the next worship service in the morning.

As her friend turned to go, Rachel reached for her rake. Her back warned that she shouldn't plan on working much longer, but she ignored it. She could hear the rumble of the trash truck a couple of streets away, and getting as many leaves to the street should be her mission.

Mission. She hadn't used that word for a long time. How long would it take before she could feel completely Amish? There must be a way to smother her past at the same time she built her future.

Then you could be the perfect Amish wife Isaac is looking for, she thought before she could halt it.

The urge to laugh battled with the tears filling her eyes. He considered her a *gut* candidate for his perfect wife, and she had to find a way to persuade him she wasn't. It'd be simple if she didn't want to protect their friendship. She could have told him that he was *ab in kopp* to think he could find that paragon. It'd be easy to say only a crazy man would believe such a person existed.

She didn't want to dash his hopes as her own had been when she'd discovered Travis's first love was his military career. How she'd admired that when they first met, and she'd fallen for the dedicated soldier! She couldn't fault him. He'd never pretended to be something he wasn't.

As she was.

No! She was a plain *mamm* with two sweet daughters who wanted to help in the recovery of the flood-torn village. What she'd been in the past was in the past. What she was now was what she wanted to be in the future, but she was struggling to find her way each day.

Which made her the worst choice for Isaac to marry.

She sighed. Having her thoughts go around and around

wasn't leading her to a solution of the problem of how to keep Isaac from broaching the subject of marriage.

As if thinking his name caused him to appear, Isaac strode along the street. He carried his toolbox in one hand and had a step stool balanced over his opposite shoulder.

"Some of you look as if you're having fun," he called as he set the box and the stool not far from where she'd raked the leaves onto the street.

She paused and leaned on her rake. Aware of how her hair was poking out in every direction from beneath the black kerchief she wore on her head, she resisted pushing it in place. That could make him think that she cared about what he thought of how she looked.

"Some of us are having more fun than others," she replied.

"I can see that." He lifted the girls out of the leaves Rachel had gathered near the sidewalk. Leaves were scattered around what had been a neat pile.

Her daughters protested but Isaac murmured something to them, and they nodded before they ran across the yard. Their steps jolted the kitten awake, and the three began chasing each other in a merry game.

After Isaac had carried his tools to a clear spot on the lawn, Rachel asked, "What did you say to them? I can't get them to quiet that quickly."

"I told them if they helped instead of sending the leaves in every direction, I'd take them for ice cream." Smiling, he added, "I may have suggested as well that the sooner the task here was done, the sooner we could have ice cream."

"Bribery!"

"It's a time-honored parenting skill that I learned while dealing with my younger brothers and Abby."

She wanted to ask him why his voice always had that

undercurrent of regret and sorrow when he spoke of his youth. It couldn't have been because he believed he'd done something wrong in helping his widowed *daed*. Was Isaac ashamed his *daed* had a weakness for alcohol?

He wants a perfect wife. Maybe he wanted a perfect daed, *too.* The thought struck her like a blow from her *daed*'s hand. So often she'd heard others state—teasing, but with the assurance of honesty—how Isaac wanted each step of the building process to be perfect before going on to the next.

Maybe she was, she realized for the first time, dodging a bullet not to meet the qualifications he was seeking in a wife.

No! she thought as she had before. Isaac wasn't unbending. He smiled and made a few jokes at his own expense. He was kindhearted and treated her girls, even Loribeth, who avoided him as much as possible, with a gentle humor that impressed her. Abby, who was an amazing woman, had said more than once how much she'd learned from Isaac.

She was right back where she'd started, trying to figure out a way to keep him from asking her to be his wife, so they could remain friends. If she only knew how…

"Hey!" he shouted as he sped toward the road where her daughters had chased the kitten.

An explosion cut through the air. A roar reverberated through her body. She was thrown into a moment she'd tried never to recall. A moment of useless destruction. Of grief. Of death.

She screamed.

Isaac froze and so did the two little girls as they skidded to a stop next to the piles of leaves at the edge of the yard. Stunned by the shriek that must have been torn from Rachel's throat, he looked from her shocked *kinder* to where she crouched with her arms flung over her head.

"Mamm!" cried Loribeth, racing past him.

He grabbed Eva and ran. He passed Loribeth in a few steps, but slowed as he reached Rachel, who was making sounds that he wasn't sure were words or groans. He couldn't understand anything she said.

"Watch your sister," he ordered as he set Eva on her feet.

Loribeth opened her mouth to protest, but he gave her a swift look that silenced her. She took Eva by the hand and leaned her cheek on her *mamm*'s shoulder.

Rachel flinched away.

The little girl's eyes filled with tears, and Eva began to cry.

Though he wanted to comfort them, he needed to see to Rachel first. He kneeled beside her, ignoring the rumble of the trash truck as it stopped at the edge of the yard.

Not touching her, he whispered, "Rachel."

She didn't react.

He spoke her name again and again, and on the fourth try, she raised her head. Her face was colorless. She blinked as if waking from a long and horrible nightmare.

"Isaac?" Her voice cracked on his name. "What are you doing here? You shouldn't be…" She looked around, her eyes widening as she took in the autumnal scene and the trash truck moving along the street to the next yard. "Oh."

She didn't add anything more as he put his hands under her elbows and brought her to her feet. The girls were silent when he gestured for them to lead the way toward their front door.

Seating her on the steps, he poured out a cup of some juice from the jug Eva tried to heft. He gave the girls each a paper cup, too, but neither of them took a sip as they stared at their *mamm*. Did they have any idea of what was going on? He guessed the answer was no.

So what *had* happened to make Rachel cry out like she had? Not just today, but that day a few weeks ago in the community center, when she'd cowered in the pantry.

"Danki," Rachel whispered as she took the cup he handed her. She sipped, then put it beside her. "That's disgusting." A faint smile warmed her too-gray skin.

"Mamm?" asked Loribeth.

"Ja?"

The little girl hesitated, but her younger sister didn't. "Okay, *Mamm*?"

Rachel curved her hands around each of her daughters' faces. "I will be. Don't worry."

Not soothed by her *mamm*'s words, Loribeth asked the question Isaac wanted to ask. "What happened?"

"I saw— That is, I thought I saw something scary." Her warm smile must have cost her dearly because it wavered as she said, "I was wrong. I'm sorry I frightened you. Go and get Sweetie Pie. It's going to be time to start supper soon."

He wasn't sure if the girls would obey, but after a moment, they scurried away. As soon as they reached the kitten, they began to giggle, their fears forgotten.

It wouldn't be that easy for either Rachel or him.

He held the door open as she went inside. He didn't wait for an invitation to follow once the girls returned, Loribeth carrying the kitten. When he suggested they take Sweetie Pie to their room to play, they glanced at Rachel. Not for permission, he was certain, but to make sure their *mamm* wasn't going to collapse again in front of their eyes.

Rachel sat in the rocker while he went outside. He collected her rake and his tools. After putting them by the front steps, he brought the jug of juice inside with him. He glanced at where she was rocking. When she didn't speak, he went into the kitchen and put the teakettle on without saying anything, either.

As sounds of childish glee came from the girls' bedroom, he sat on the sofa. He turned his gaze to Rachel, who was staring straight ahead. "You're acting like a friend of mine."

"How?" Her voice was cautious, as if she'd weighed the simplest word before she let it leave her lips.

"Any loud sound terrified him." When she glanced at him, he held her gaze. "He was in a buggy that was hit by a train when he was a *kind*. His parents were killed, and he never could endure any loud sound. His *doktor* called it post-traumatic something or other."

"Post-traumatic stress disorder," she whispered.

"*Ja*, that's it." His eyebrows lowered. "I'm surprised you know about it."

"I've read about it in the newspapers."

"I have, too. Soldiers coming home from wars and being unable to forget what they've seen and heard." He shook his head. "It made me realize we must continue to pray for them when the wars aren't in the newspapers every day."

"*Ja*."

He waited for her to add more, but she didn't. Instead, she stood and went to remove the teakettle when it began to whistle. She poured hot water into two cups and then dropped a tea bag in each one. After handing him one, she sat in the rocker.

When he held the cup close to his nose, he smelled the distinct sharpness of mint. That was unexpected, but after taking a sip, he realized she'd picked the perfect flavor.

It was warming and cooling at the same time. He sipped and waited. He'd said all he could.

"I saw a *gut* friend killed," she said, "and though I don't think about it every minute of every day any longer, the memory lurks. Any loud noise, especially any unexpected noise, resurrects that moment and how powerless I was to save his life."

"I'm sorry, Rachel."

She reached across the small space between them and touched his arm so fleetingly he almost believed he'd imagined her light caress. "*Danki*, but I've learned it's futile to try to change the past. I'm sure you understand that."

"I do indeed," he replied, though he doubted she could guess how sincerely he meant those words.

The two little girls burst into the room, wearing eager expressions. Eva rushed to him and tugged on his sleeve.

"Ice keem!" Eva exclaimed. "'Member? Ice keem?"

"*Ja*, I do 'member," he said, relieved for the chance to put aside the awful topic and smile at the *kind* whose greatest concern was whether he'd do as he promised and treat her and her sister to ice cream. "Shall we go to the diner and see what flavors they've got tonight?"

Rachel began, "If you three want to—"

"They serve ice cream to quartets," he said. Setting his cup on the counter, he offered her his hand. "*Komm mol*, Rachel. You can't prefer mint tea to chocolate ice cream."

"Choco." Eva spoke the word as if it was the sweetest one in the world.

Rachel looked from him to her daughters. Though Loribeth had been silent, anticipation glistened in her eyes.

Letting him bring her to her feet, she smiled at her girls. "Maybe they have mint chocolate chip, ain't so?"

"Who knows?" He took her cup and set it next to his.

She sent her daughters to get their coats and bonnets, then faced him. *"Danki."*

"It does get better. That's what my friend told me."

"I keep reminding myself of that. Days and weeks go by, and everything is fine until…"

"Don't think about it any more today."

"You're right. Let's enjoy our 'ice keem.'"

As she herded the girls ahead of her, he noticed her trembling hands. No other sign of her despair was visible in how she chatted with the girls about which flavor they would order.

He shivered as he stepped outside, though the afternoon remained warm. He thought of how vulnerable she'd looked while huddled on the ground, her hands over her head. Whatever had happened to her must have been horrific.

If there's a way to ease her path away from that appalling memory, Lord, guide me to it.

She was a strong woman. That was one of the criteria on his list for his perfect wife. Would he ever meet anyone—man or woman—stronger than Rachel? So when was he going to match her courage and ask her to be his wife? As he watched her holding the girls' hands and swinging them as they walked along, he knew it had to be soon.

Chapter Eleven

Rachel opened her wallet and put two dimes on the counter at the rear of the general store. That paid for the penny candy she'd let her girls pick out after more than five minutes of discussion.

"Thank you for your patience, Mrs. Weiskopf," Rachel said to the elderly woman behind the counter.

"I know how important such a choice is when you're their age," the white-haired woman said with a smile. "Every child wants to sample as many different items as they can. That's why we've kept the penny candy counter open, though there's no profit in it. Sometimes, it's not about money. Sometimes, it's about memories."

"You're right," she replied, though she would have been as happy to forget most of what had happened while she was a *kind*. "Got your bags, girls?"

Loribeth held up her small white bag, but Eva was too busy looking into hers to pay attention.

Thanking Mrs. Weiskopf, Rachel took her daughters by the hands and led them toward the door.

The breeze had a wintry chill in it when they stepped out onto the porch. She felt her daughters shiver and squatted to button their coats. The sun had been shining when they went inside, but storm clouds roiled over the mountains. Glancing toward the bridge, she saw several silhouettes moving in its direction. She wondered how long it would take before the hint of rain sent chills, icier than the autumnal wind, through the residents of the small town.

Movement on the sidewalk caught her eye. She looked away, then back so swiftly her bonnet bounced. Every inch of her tensed with a fear greater and older than what she'd endured when the sound of the trash truck hitting a pothole had resurrected the memory of death and destruction in the desert.

A pair of men were walking toward the store. They hadn't reached the steps that had been replaced after the flood and were raw lumber. Both wore black coats and broadfall trousers. Only one had a beard, and it fell to his chest, but it couldn't hide the deep chasm of a scar on his left cheek. He was gesticulating as he said something to the man striding alongside him.

She looked away, telling herself she had to be mistaken. There must be hundreds of plain men who wore long, pewter-gray beards and gestured vehemently with their hands. And the scar from the corner of his eye to his lips? There had to be other men with similar gouges in their faces.

That couldn't be her *daed*!

Not in Evergreen Corners, a place where she was sure she'd be safe from his unstable temper.

When Loribeth started to ask a question, she silenced her girls by urging them to select one piece of candy each from their bags. That kept them occupied while the two men walked by, not glancing in her direction. But she saw enough of the older man's face to know the truth.

It was her *daed*! What was Manassas Yoder doing here?

Grateful her bonnet concealed so much of her face, she waited for the men to turn onto the street that led across the bridge. She steered her daughters up the hill. Panic gripped her, making it hard to breathe. Where should she go? If *Daed* had seen her, he could follow her home. She didn't want to be alone with the man who had punished her and her siblings for the slightest infraction. What would her military friends think of her if they saw her fleeing like a frightened rabbit from a bent old man?

What would her friends in Evergreen Corners think of her avoiding her *daed*?

What would Isaac think?

Somehow, while trying not to consider the answers to those questions, Rachel got through the rest of the afternoon until she could concentrate on making supper for her small family. She pushed the close encounter from her head and began to hope that her *daed* hadn't seen her. Evergreen Corners was at a crossroads of two major routes in Vermont. Maybe it was only by chance her *daed* had walked by the store.

She couldn't believe that. Her family lived in Ohio, and she couldn't imagine a single reason her *daed* would be in town other than she was there. She'd been foolish to believe Evergreen Corners could become a haven while she regained the equilibrium to go on with her life. She was no closer to returning to the woman she used to be before tragedy tore apart her life. She'd seen that when she'd overreacted last week to the sound of a backfiring trash truck.

Dear God, show me Your mercy and help me protect my daughters.

She stirred spaghetti sauce on the stove, then wiped her hands on her apron. Stepping around Sweetie Pie, she took out a box of spaghetti. She gave a single piece to each girl and urged them to use them to play with the kitten in the living room. Soon the *kinder* were squealing with delight as Sweetie Pie tried to capture the tip of the spaghetti. They were kept busy until she'd finished preparing their supper. After they shared a silent prayer, the girls ate while Rachel pushed her food around her plate, unable to swallow a single bite.

At a knock at the door, everything stopped for Rachel. She had no thoughts. She couldn't move. She felt nothing but fear.

Loribeth jumped to her feet and raced to the door.

She wanted to halt her daughter, but couldn't make a sound. She watched, helpless as a newborn *boppli*, as the little girl swung open the door, then slammed it shut.

"It's *him*." The disgust in Loribeth's voice broke through Rachel's paralysis. Her daughter used that tone only when speaking of Isaac.

Relief and happiness flooded Rachel. Her *daed* wasn't on her front steps. Standing, she drew in a slow, steadying breath and managed to make her feet work enough to carry her to the door.

When she reopened the door, she looked into Isaac's warm smile and knew that while her relief was because Manassas Yoder wasn't there, her happiness was because Isaac *was*. Before she spoke a single word, she knew Isaac would offer her well-thought-out advice if she told him about her *daed*.

Thoughts of Manassas Yoder fled from her mind as she savored the sight of Isaac on her doorstep. His brown eyes were twinkling with *gut* humor. He wore a white shirt beneath the black suspenders that emphasized the breadth of his shoulders.

Her eyes widened when she realized he held some

gold-and-orange mums. When he handed the bouquet to her, she smiled.

"Does this mean what I think it means?" she asked.

"What do you think it means?"

"You've put an offer on the farm. You wouldn't have picked the mums by the house's porch otherwise, ain't so?"

His smile wobbled for a moment, then strengthened. "I can never surprise you, can I, Rachel? You see right through me."

"Oh, how *wunderbaar*!"

"That I'm that obvious?"

"No." She let him into the house. "That you've put in an offer on the farm. Abby must be thrilled, too."

"I'm sure she'll be, assuming the deal goes through."

Asking him questions about what would happen next with his offer, she listened to his answers as she led the way into the kitchen. She filled a glass and carried it into the dining room. She put the flowers in it, smiling as her daughters grinned at the bright blossoms. Her fingers trembled so much that water spilled on the table. She rushed to get a cloth.

"What's wrong?" Isaac asked as he followed her into the kitchen, and she knew his keen eyes hadn't missed how her hands shook.

She didn't dissemble because she knew the answer to one of her questions. She wanted to tell Isaac what had happened and get his insight into her quandary. "I think I saw my *daed* today in Evergreen Corners."

"You think? You didn't go and speak with him?"

She shook her head. "No. After I first ran away years ago, he told me that if I ever defied him and left again, he never wanted anything to do with me."

"Words said in anger aren't always what someone feels."

"I know, but in this case, he meant every syllable." She sighed as she looked toward the living room. "I didn't want the girls to be present if he got angry, as he did so often when I was young."

"You can't avoid him forever, Rachel. He's your *daed*, and you must be the reason he's come to Evergreen Corners."

"I don't know why he's here. I left home over twenty years ago. He never came looking for me."

"He never *found* you, you mean. You don't know how long he's been looking for you. It might have been from the day you left."

Rachel shook her head. She didn't want to listen to Isaac's usual *gut* sense. To allow herself to imagine *Daed* had been searching for her since she left home would suggest he cared about her other than as an extra pair of hands to help around the farm. If he had, why hadn't he shown that to her at least once during the seventeen years she'd lived at home?

As if in answer to her unspoken question, an assertive knock sounded on the front door. Her defenses rose, as she prepared to use the skills that had kept her alive while deployed. She calculated what would be the best and safest course of action. First, she called out to her girls to stay where they were.

Standing on tiptoe, she peeked out the window over the sink. She could barely see the front steps, but in the last of the twilight, she discovered not one, but two silhouettes there.

Isaac matched her motion. "Is one of them your *daed*?"

"I think so."

"You should talk with him, Rachel. You need to find out why he's come to Evergreen Corners."

"I don't know if—"

Another knock sounded.

"Do you want me to answer it?" he asked.

With all my heart, she longed to say, but she shook her head. If her *daed* was out there, she couldn't use Isaac as a human shield against him.

Telling the girls again to stay where they were, she rushed to the door. She had to unfold her fingers, which were closed in fists, before she could open it. Seeking out to God in silent prayer to be with her, she threw open the door.

She stared. The man next to her *daed* was as familiar to her as her reflection in a mirror. He was taller than she remembered him, but the bright blue eyes in his rugged face identified him as her younger brother, Robert. She could recall the days he and their sister, Arlene, had been born. Like her, as they grew up, they were made to feel worthless.

"Do you recognize me, Rachel?" he asked, his voice far deeper than the one in her memory.

"Ja." She wanted to throw her arms wide and welcome her brother into her life, but she couldn't be unaware of the man standing beside him. "How are you, Robbie?"

"I'm *gut*. How are you, Rachel?"

She started to reply *gut*, but paused, not wanting to ply her brother with a lie. "Surprised. I'm surprised to see you here, Robbie."

"Robert," he corrected. "I go by Robert now. *Daed* says a grown man shouldn't have a *kind*'s name."

"How did you find me?"

"One of the scribes for *The Budget* mentioned the volunteers working here. Your name was included. When someone showed it to *Daed*, he insisted we come here."

Why hadn't she considered the possibility that someone among the plain community would have written regular letters about the flood-recovery efforts to *The Budget*, the newspaper that connected plain people around the world? She'd become too complacent, hadn't been looking over her shoulder every minute as she had when she first moved into the *Englisch* world.

Her brother cleared his throat, then asked, "May we come in? Both of us?"

The words that he was welcome to enter her home, but *Daed* was not, burned on her tongue. She almost spoke them. She halted herself when she felt small hands on her skirt as Eva tried to peer past her, curious to see who was at the door.

"I don't know," she said.

"He's changed, Rachel."

"Are you sure?" She wanted to bite back the words bursting from her foolish heart. She wanted to believe it was possible to have the *daed* she'd always wanted. How many times had she listened to her heart and returned home? Too many, and each time it had betrayed her.

"Since *Mamm* died, he's been nicer to us."

"*Mamm* died?" Tears welled in her eyes, startling her. She'd wished her *mamm* had been strong enough to step between her husband and their *kinder* when he lost his temper and struck out at them. Even so, she'd loved her *mamm* deeply.

"About two years ago. She died in her sleep." Robert gave her a sad smile. "Peacefully." *Unlike how she'd lived*. Her brother didn't say the words, but she heard them in her heart. "Can we come in?"

Like before, she knew she must not make a scene in

front of her daughters. It would be better, as Isaac had suggested, to talk with her *daed* and listen to what he'd come to say. After that, she could decide what to do about speaking with him in the future.

"Of course," she said. "*Komm* in."

She stepped aside to let the men in, then edged away another involuntary pace when her *daed* entered her home. Suddenly she felt as young and weak as the *kind* who'd endured his temper.

A hand at the center of her back kept her from continuing to distance herself from the man who'd made her childhood a nightmare. At the touch, her heart skittered within her. Isaac! She wasn't facing her *daed* alone. Her panic ebbed for the first time since she'd first seen her *daed* that afternoon. One of the first lessons she'd learned in the Army was the strength there was in having someone at your side you could depend on. And she could depend on Isaac.

Daed looked older than the image she'd been carrying in her head. With a start of amazement, she realized she was approaching the age he'd been when she'd left home for the final time. He must be in his late sixties now, and his strong nose and narrowed eyes were flanked by thick valleys of wrinkles.

He rolled the brim of his black church hat in his hands as he paused in the middle of her living room. His bushy gray eyebrows lowered when he noted the two little girls standing beside her and Isaac behind her.

"Your family?" her *daed* asked in a creaking voice.

"The girls are my daughters. Isaac is another of the volunteers in Evergreen Corners." She wished she could steal a glance at Isaac to discover what he was thinking about her *daed*.

"You found someone to marry you?"

"Ja." She fought not to bristle at the question that suggested whoever had been willing to wed her must have been a *dummkopf* of the first order. "We were married for almost six years."

"Where is your husband?"

"He died."

Her *daed*'s eyebrows arched, but for once he didn't make the snide comment she'd expected. When he mumbled something that might have been "I'm sorry," she was startled. Could Robbie—Robert—have been right? Had their *daed* changed?

"As I said, these are my daughters." She put a hand on each girl's shoulder as she said their names and ages.

"They favor you."

"I see their *daed* in them, as well." To her daughters, she added, "This is your *grossdawdi*." When the girls gave her puzzled looks, she bent to whisper in each one's ear. "Your grandpa." A quick glance toward the men showed that none of them had heard her speak the *Englisch* word so the girls would understand the stranger in front of them was her *daed*. "This is Robert." She smiled, though the expression felt alien on her lips when she stood in the same room as Manassas Yoder. "He's my little brother."

Eva tilted her head to gaze at Robert. "You no little. Me little."

"I used to be little but I grew."

"Me, too?" Eva spun to face Rachel. "Me grow, too? No little no more?"

"Ja," she said, stroking her *kind*'s cheek, "but promise you won't grow up too fast."

"It's not our way," *Daed* interrupted, "to make promises. That's something you should be teaching your *kinder*, Rachel." Glancing around the trailer, he wrinkled his nose. "It's not right, raising them among these *Englischers*."

Isaac cleared his throat, then said, "We have a growing plain community here in Evergreen Corners. There are more than thirty plain people here."

"All Amish?"

"Some are Mennonite, but our numbers fluctuate as people come and go. Most have homes they must keep an eye on as well as volunteering here."

"They should be with their real family. They have an *aenti* and *onkels* as well as several cousins."

"What?" asked Loribeth. "We've got what?"

Sorrow erupted through Rachel as *Daed* went on to list the names of Arlene's eight *kinder*. The girls spoke *Deitsch* with ease, but they didn't know the words for their relatives other than *mamm* and *daed*, because she'd never used them with Loribeth and Eva.

To cover her daughter's furtive whisper, Rachel said more loudly, "Girls, you should say hello to your *grossdawdi*."

"Hello," the girls said.

"*Komm* here." *Daed* sat on the sofa and patted his knee.

Both girls wrapped their arms around Rachel and clung to her.

He scowled, and his eyes slitted as he looked at Rachel. His expression told her that he—again—found her lacking.

"They're shy," Isaac said in the quiet tone that warned he wouldn't be budged by argument from anyone. "Perhaps it'd be better if you talked to them from where you are on this first meeting."

"They're my *kins-kinder*!" he retorted.

"True, but you're a stranger to them. You need to give them time to get to know you."

"You're right, Isaac," her *daed* said, shocking her. She couldn't remember him backing down when someone suggested he was wrong.

Had he really changed? After all, she was different from the young girl who'd jumped the fence, believing everything she wanted and needed was in the *Englisch* world.

"Give the girls some time," Isaac urged. "It's taken them a while to get used to us in Evergreen Corners, but they've come around."

"We can stay for only a few days," Robert said, speaking to Rachel for the first time since they'd come inside.

Rachel made a decision. "*Komm* to supper tomorrow night." By then, she might be prepared to deal with a *daed* who'd found ways to control his temper. She couldn't let her heart betray her into foolishness.

Her gaze slipped toward Isaac. No, she must not let her heart and her longing to belong to a family delude her again.

Isaac tried to ignore his relief when Rachel's *daed* and brother left. Though she'd warned him about how uneasy she was about speaking with Manassas, he'd been shocked that she tiptoed around the man. She'd tried to hide how she flinched whenever he raised his voice, but he'd seen it. Had her *daed*?

Her brother seemed to be a decent man, but was almost as tentative around Manassas as Rachel was. The reactions told Isaac there was more to the story than an Amish patriarch being furious when one of his *kinder* decided not to be baptized and ran away to live among *Englischers*.

Guilt clawed at him when he realized he was grateful that their arrival tonight must have dimmed Rachel's memory of him bringing her flowers. He'd never guessed her first thoughts would be of him and his dream. He'd hoped the flowers would open the door to a conversation about her becoming his wife, but that hadn't happened.

He wasn't being fair, he reminded himself as he stood in the doorway to the girls' bedroom. Rachel had been unnerved by seeing her *daed*. Tonight hadn't been the right night to initiate a discussion. He had to have faith a better opportunity was waiting.

"He's really and truly your *daed*?" asked Loribeth as Rachel bent to tuck her into bed.

"*Ja*, he is, and he's your *grossdawdi*."

The little girl wore a puzzled frown. "He went away, and he came back. Will my *daed* come back, too?"

When Rachel blinked hard, he guessed she was trying not to cry. She sat on the side of Loribeth's bed. He looked at where Eva was listening from the other bed and knew Rachel had to choose her words with care. As if for the first time, he realized what a hard task she had of raising two little girls alone.

He admired her strength as she forced a smile that looked genuine enough to comfort the *kinder*. Knowing how much each motion was costing her, he watched as she bent to kiss Loribeth's forehead.

"No, your *daed* won't be coming back." Her voice softened to a tender whisper. "Remember? Your *daed* is with God, and he's waiting for us when it's our turn to—"

"To meet God," Isaac quickly interjected when her voice faded into uncertain silence. She was, he knew, struggling not to cause the youngsters more pain.

She never spoke of how her husband had died. Isaac

had no idea if the man had been ill or if there had been a terrible accident.

"That's right," Rachel said, drawing his attention to her. "You must wait until God calls you home."

"Until then," Isaac said, "it's important you treat others with kindness and be *gut* girls who listen to your *mamm.*"

"Even Alyssa?" asked Loribeth, shocking him because she'd avoided speaking to him. The girls were as distressed as their *mamm* over the unexpected guests this evening.

Though he had no idea who Alyssa was, Isaac said, "*Ja*, you must treat Alyssa with kindness."

"She broke my blue crayon and told Miss Gwen I did it."

"That wasn't nice, ain't so?" he asked.

The girls shook their heads.

"Some people aren't as nice as they should be, but that means we need to be nice ourselves, so they can see how they're supposed to behave."

"Oh," Loribeth said, her eyes widening. "Like being a roller mob-el?"

"Ja." He glanced at Rachel, who was fighting a smile, though her eyes glistened with unshed tears. "At least I think so."

Standing, Rachel smoothed the covers. "*Ja*, you need to be a role model like Miss Gwen says."

"Okay," the little girl said, but didn't appear persuaded.

"'Kay," her sister said, then added, "And forgive, ain't so, I-zak?"

"Ja." He wondered if Eva had any idea what it meant to forgive…or if he did.

He ignored thoughts of his own *daed* while Rachel

said a prayer with the girls and gave them each another kiss before turning on their night-lights. She closed their door after checking the kitten was napping on the kitchen floor, one paw pinning down a piece of uncooked spaghetti.

"Kaffi?" she asked as they went into the kitchen.

"Not for me. Get some for yourself if you want."

"I don't think I need caffeine tonight."

He translated that to mean she was already too on edge to sleep. Or maybe she wanted to be alone to sort out what had happened that day. Her life had been upended, and she must need time in prayer to seek guidance for how to handle tomorrow night's conversation with her brother and *daed*.

"I should be going," he said, though he wanted to remain and offer what help he could.

"You're welcome to join us tomorrow for supper." She took a breath and let it go. "I'd like you to come tomorrow night, Isaac, but I'll understand if you don't want to."

"I'll be there."

Her shoulders sagged with relief. *"Danki,* Isaac."

"I enjoy coming to your table."

"My thanks isn't for that," she said as he reached for the doorknob. "Loribeth's question threw me for a loop."

"Having your *daed* here tonight has rattled you." Before he could halt himself, he brushed a strand of her ebony hair toward her *kapp*, curling it behind her ear. His fingers lingered for a moment, then he drew them away.

How he longed to touch her soft cheek and tilt her mouth toward his! He couldn't guess anything else that would have been more foolish. He wished her pleasant dreams and let himself out before he gave in to his yearning to kiss her.

Something had gone wrong with his plan for finding the perfect wife. He was falling in love with Rachel Yoder, and that could make him as witless as his *daed* had been after *Mamm*'s death.

As he hurried across the deserted village green, he knew Rachel wouldn't be the only one reaching out to God tonight. He needed help himself before he lost his head and, for the first time in longer than he could recall, listened first to his heart.

Chapter Twelve

Pausing by the table that was set for six, Rachel hoped *Daed* would appreciate how much work her daughters had done to make it special for him. They'd made cards from folded sheets of construction paper and pictures they'd cut out of magazines at the day-care center. Loribeth had been able to sign her name, but Eva drew a pair of stick figures that were supposed to be her and her *grossdawdi*. A sun shone in the sky above their heads, a sign that Eva believed made it a happy scene.

Rachel wanted to believe it'd be a joyous reunion tonight. She longed to believe her *daed* had changed as much as she had during the past two decades. When she'd left home, she couldn't have imagined she'd find a career in the Army, marry and have *kinder* and find her way back to a plain life. If someone had told her what path her life would take, she would have laughed, saying it was impossible.

But it had happened, and she was in Evergreen Corners, Vermont, ready to offer her *daed* a home-cooked meal.

Her uncertainty must have infected her daughters because the girls were subdued while she helped them dress for the meal, which was cooking in the oven. They hadn't pleaded to sample the cake she'd baked earlier, and she wasn't sure if she'd heard them speak much above a whisper all day. Sweetie Pie had been ignored except when Loribeth had fallen asleep after day care on the couch with the kitten curled into the curve of her body.

"You look *wunderbaar*," she said as she smiled at her daughters.

"Cute as a button," Loribeth replied. "That's what Miss Gwen says. Why are buttons cute, *Mamm*?"

"I don't know. Plain women don't use them, ain't so?"

"Cute as a pin?" asked Eva, looking at the ones holding Rachel's apron in place.

Hugging her daughters, Rachel sent up a prayer of gratitude for these two precious gifts God had given her. She would have done anything for them, and hosting her *daed* tonight was proof of that.

She left the girls to their coloring books while she oversaw supper. She was making scalloped potatoes and pork chops. The casserole was in the oven, and she had green beans waiting to be cooked on top. Chowchow and applesauce were already on the table. She would put the rolls in to warm while she served the rest of the food, and planned to bring them and butter and apple butter to the table once the water for the beans was set to boil.

It was a meal *Mamm* had made for special occasions. The thought of her *mamm* having died without Rachel being able to say goodbye staggered her, especially when she realized her death and Travis's must have been within months of each other. If God had been making sure the news was postponed so she had no more pain than she could handle as her life was turned inside out, she was grateful to Him. She'd felt so alone in the wake of Travis's death, having a young *kind* and pregnant with another.

You don't have to be alone. The words whispered in her head. If only she could be the wife Isaac wanted, the wife he deserved...

Rachel focused on supper preparations to halt her thoughts. She poured sweet cider that one of the volunteers had brought from his orchard to share. Arranging the glasses on the counter, she checked she had milk for Eva, who didn't like cider. When a knock sounded on the door, she was taking the lid off the casserole so the pork chops would brown during the last fifteen minutes of cooking. She set it on the stove and went to answer the door. She shot her daughters a smile when they began collecting their crayons and books and putting them in the toy cubby by the sofa.

Opening the door, she smiled at Robert and their *daed*. They were dressed in their Sunday best, and she was glad that she also had chosen the light blue dress she wore to worship services.

"*Komm* in," she urged. "It's getting chillier with every passing evening."

Her daughters scurried to her side, their eyes wide as they stared at the men. Robert bent to greet them, but *Daed* strode past everyone and looked into the dining room.

Facing her, he asked, "Why is the table set for six?"

"Isaac is joining us, too."

"Are you walking out with him?"

She hesitated, unsure why she'd heard what sounded like venom in her *daed*'s voice. Why would he speak so of Isaac? They'd met briefly. Had *Daed* taken offense when Isaac's comment made him admit he was mistaken?

Glancing at her brother, she saw he was as bothered by their *daed*'s tone as she was. That made her more ill at ease.

"No, we aren't walking out together," she replied, as if there hadn't been a break in the conversation. "Isaac is, as I said, another volunteer in the recovery efforts. He's been kind to us as have the rest of the plain folks—as well as the *Englischers*—in town."

He gave her a quelling scowl, but she didn't cower as she had in the past. She'd had too many other frowns aimed in her direction when she'd given orders to her transportation company that weren't popular. Looks couldn't kill, though there had been plenty of other ways for the people under her command to die.

She squelched the shiver racing along her spine. She needed to keep her mind from the past. She couldn't change it.

"*Daed*, would you like some cider?" she asked in a tone she hoped sounded cheerful.

Before he could answer, a knock at the door announced Isaac had arrived. She thrust one of the glasses of cider into her *daed*'s hand, urged him and her brother to sit in the living room, and turned to get the door.

Her smile widened at the sight of Isaac on the steps. He, too, was dressed in his *mutze* coat and dark pants, and she wondered if he'd ever looked more handsome than he did when he whispered, "Am I on time?"

"You're here at the perfect time." She realized what she'd said and wanted to take back the words in case Isaac thought she was making fun of him and his quest for a perfect wife.

"*Gut.*"

Leaving him to talk to Robert, *Daed* and the girls, she rushed into the kitchen to finish preparing the food. Her fingers were clumsy as she worked and listened to the stilted conversation from the other room. She didn't shoo away her daughters when they came in to be with her.

In spite of having to walk around them each time she moved, she got supper on the table. She swung Eva onto the bench, where she'd sit, too, and moved Loribeth's chair to her other side. Calling to the men to join them, she motioned for each of them to take a seat.

Robert chose the chair across from her when *Daed* pulled out the one at the head of the table, next to where Loribeth sat. That left the one next to Eva for Isaac, who asked her *daed* to lead them in silent prayer.

She took her daughters' hands and bowed her head. She raised it when her *daed* bumped his knee against the table leg, the sign he'd always used to announce he was done. Serving the little girls and cutting their food into bite-size pieces, she was kept busy while the men spooned out the fragrant casserole and passed around vegetables and rolls.

Isaac turned the conversation to the work the volunteers had been doing for almost a year in Evergreen Corners. Her brother had a lot of questions, and the two men soon were talking as if they'd been friends for years. *Daed* didn't speak often unless he was asking for more food to be passed to him. Keeping her girls quiet and eating occupied Rachel.

Conversation halted as if a switch had been flipped when her *daed* held out his hand to her older daughter. "*Komm* here, girl."

Loribeth shrank away from her *grossdawdi*'s outstretched hand and giggled nervously.

"They're bashful," Robert said in a consoling tone. "Remember? Isaac mentioned that last night."

Daed glared at Rachel, who was trying to divert Loribeth into eating the rest of her roll spread with apple butter. "I suppose you've been telling them more of your made-up stories about your pitiful childhood, so they hate me."

"I've never said a word about it to them," Rachel said quietly.

"I'm sure you've told him." *Daed* flung a hand in Isaac's direction and made a baleful sound deep in his throat. "You never could keep your mouth closed about private family business."

"I haven't said anything to anyone," she said as Loribeth put her hand over her mouth, but began to laugh when Eva did. Rachel was sure the girls didn't find anything funny about the situation, but they didn't know how else to react to their *grossdawdi* growling like a rabid dog.

"Why should I believe that when my *kins-kinder* avoid me? You've lied all your life, daughter."

She hadn't. She'd always been honest with him, and during her childhood, that had enraged him more. She sought an answer that wouldn't set him off, but she delayed too long.

Daed surged to his feet, and she was again the frightened little girl she'd been. She was facing a tyrannical parent and fearing she'd suffer the back of his hand or the lash of his belt. She cowered, unable to halt herself, when he reached toward her.

Then she realized he wasn't interested in her. He glowered at Loribeth as he said, "Stop that infernal giggling, girl!"

"Her name is Loribeth," Rachel said, trying to batten down her instinctive fear. She wasn't that helpless *kind* any longer. She was a woman who'd been taught, through the tough lessons of boot camp and deployments, to remain calm when facing her enemies.

Was that how she thought of her *daed*? As the enemy? She shouldn't—

That thought was interrupted when he snarled, "She needs to do as she's told. Every *kind* needs to learn to obey its elders." He grabbed Loribeth's arm and jerked her out of her chair.

The little girl screeched more in surprise than in pain, but Rachel knew how it would go. First horrible words spewing from her *daed*'s mouth, words aimed at tearing her apart, and then would come the blows.

Every ounce of her rebelled against him inflicting his idea of parenting on her *kinder*. Every moment of training she'd had in the military came to the forefront.

Standing so fast that the bench skidded backward across the floor, she stepped between Loribeth and her *daed*. She didn't raise her hand, simply bent her elbow, putting her forearm across her body. In her mind, she heard her self-defense instructor explaining the bones in her lower arm were among the strongest in her body. Her arm would help ward off a blow from any direction.

"Don't touch my *kinder*," she warned softly as she put her left hand against Loribeth's narrow chest so she could push her daughter away if necessary.

Beside her, like a miniature warrior, Sweetie Pie arched and hissed. Her fur fluffed out until she looked almost twice her tiny size.

"Step aside," *Daed* ordered. "It's clear you shouldn't be responsible for these *kinder* when you can't carry on a respectful discussion."

A gentle hand cupped her other elbow. As warmth seeped up her arm, she was grateful she wasn't alone in facing the man who'd abused her and her siblings. Isaac stood behind her, ready to get her girls to safety. That he hadn't spoken told her more than any words could. He might not approve of her taking such a defensive stance, but he wouldn't gainsay her because he was coming to understand why she'd been so upset at *Daed* returning to her life.

Robert began, *"Daed—"*

"That's right," their *daed* said. "Listen to your brother. I'm your *daed*, Rachel. You'll do as I say. Honor your *daed.*"

"I have tried to, but I'm also my *kinder*'s *mamm*, and I'll do what I must to keep them safe." She didn't let him force her into shifting her gaze away as she said, "As their *mamm*, I'm saying you must not ever lift your hand to either of my girls. Violence isn't our way. If you lay a hand on them, I'll call the police."

"We don't bring *Englischers* into our business."

"I will when someone threatens my girls. I don't think you realize…" She swallowed hard, holding back the words she once would have spoken if someone tried to browbeat her or one of the people in her command. Those sharp retorts belonged to another life. Just as Manassas Yoder did.

Could he have any idea how much she was aching inside? She'd dared to believe her brother was right when he said that their *daed* had changed. She'd trusted the hope in her brother's eyes when he spoke of *Daed* being in control of his temper at last. She'd imagined he could be the *daed* she'd longed for when she'd been cold and scared and in pain when he banished her to the root cellar after a beating.

Rachel drew her daughters closer and put her hands on their shoulders. "You need to leave."

"So you're throwing out your *daed*?"

"Please leave," she said in the same calm voice. It took every bit of her willpower to keep it serene, but she refused to let him see how he'd crushed her hopes that he had set aside his cruelty.

He stared at her, and when she didn't shift her gaze away, he lowered his eyes. Pushing past her, he grabbed his hat. "Let's go, Robert!" He stormed out, slamming the door in his wake.

Rachel exchanged horrified glances with Isaac and Robert. Isaac's face was grim, but Robert's was filled with shame.

"I'm sorry, Rachel," her brother said as he came around the table. "I thought... That is, I never would have..." He hung his head.

Giving him a swift hug, she said, "I wanted to believe him, too, so don't blame yourself."

"If he'd hurt your girls..." He hugged her again, then he was gone, too.

Eva flung her arms around Rachel's legs and pressed her face to them. She began to cry.

Bending, Rachel picked up her younger daughter. She hoped her trembling hands wouldn't make her drop Eva. As she snuggled the *kind* close, she looked at her other daughter. Loribeth had no more color in her face than she did the day she'd thrown up on Isaac's shoes.

"Mamm..." she began, then started to sob.

Squatting in front of Loribeth, Rachel balanced Eva on her legs while she put an arm around her older daughter. Loribeth pressed against her, almost knocking her backward. Only Isaac's hand on her shoulders kept her from tipping over onto the floor.

"It's okay," Rachel murmured to her daughters as she raised her gaze toward Isaac's face.

The cold severity remained, but as she watched, it eased into a gentler expression. For the first time in her life, after a confrontation with her *daed*, she didn't feel alone. She hadn't ever believed someone beyond her equally helpless brother and sister could be on her side, and she treasured the moment in the most secret place of her heart, where she'd been trying to hide her growing love for Isaac from herself.

Isaac watched Rachel and her *kinder*, and another wave of anger surged over him. He had fought to keep from lashing out at Manassas Yoder. Though the man had left, rage still bristled along Isaac's skin like an itch he mustn't scratch.

He said little while Rachel served slices of chocolate cake with scoops of ice cream. He barely tasted the few bites he managed to swallow.

When she gave the girls a bath and put them to bed, he was surprised Loribeth didn't shy away from him. She must have been more frightened by her *grossdawdi* than he'd guessed. Another rumble of ire resonated through him, but he silenced it, not wanting to upset the girls more.

He offered to help Rachel clear the table once the girls were in bed, but she waved aside his offer and walked into the living room. When he joined her there, she faced him. "I'm sorry, Isaac. I know I shouldn't have confronted him as I did."

"Turning the other cheek isn't easy, especially when doing so leaves your *kinder* in danger." He cupped her chin and tilted her face toward him. "Rachel, you didn't strike your *daed* or raise your voice to him. I can't say I could have spoken with such serenity if I'd been in your place."

"When I get angry, I get quict." She gave him a smile filled with regret. "That's something everyone who's ever known me has had to learn."

"I'll keep that in mind." His fingers played along her cheek, savoring the texture of her silky skin.

Her eyes grew big with wonder, and he knew that she must be savoring the same luscious sensations that were trickling up his fingers. She breathed his name. Was this the right time to pull her into his arms and kiss her? To ask her to be his wife because he believed she was the perfect one for him?

No, argued his common sense. *She tossed her daed out of her home an hour ago. She isn't thinking straight right now. Neither are you.*

When he sat on the couch, he was surprised when she sat beside him. It was the first time he'd seen her choose any spot in the living room other than her beloved rocking chair.

"You should talk to Cora Miller," he said.

He saw that she recognized the name of a fellow volunteer, who'd been one of the first in Evergreen Corners to receive a new home after the flood. "Why?"

"Cora has experience with *daeds* who are bad to their *kinder*. She came here to protect her nephew and niece from theirs." He held her gaze. "You need to forgive Manassas, Rachel. Not for him, but for yourself. Carrying around anger eats at you. Besides, as we're taught, we can only hope for forgiveness if we offer it."

"Could you forgive a man like that?"

He hated the sound of bitterness in her voice, a sound he'd heard in his own too often. "I already have. My *daed* wasn't the best, either."

"Abby mentioned that he drank too much and too often."

He was startled. "Abby knew?"

"Do you think you could pull the wool over *Abby's* eyes? She doesn't miss much."

"No, she doesn't." He wondered why he'd never considered how readily Abby saw behind the facades people built to protect themselves and others. "I should thank her for keeping me in the dark, so I didn't have to worry more about her."

"I don't think you could worry more about her. Or her about you. That's what love does."

"My sister doesn't know the whole truth." He sighed and pushed himself to his feet. "Our *daed* drank every day. Sometimes he could function. Other times he couldn't, and I had to take over when he was unable to do chores. I didn't want the younger *kinder* knowing because I kept praying one day God would open *Daed*'s eyes to what he was doing to himself and us. Though it took more time than I'd ever imagined, God did reach out to *Daed*. He opened not only *Daed*'s eyes, but his heart, so the grief left by *Mamm*'s death could be replaced by love for the woman who became his wife."

"God is *gut*."

"True, but I can't help wishing He'd acted sooner. It was more than twenty years from *Mamm*'s funeral to *Daed*'s second wedding. Those years were challenging. I know there are those who say that God doesn't give us more than we can handle with His assistance, but there were times when I wanted to throw in the towel and walk away."

She folded her hands as if in prayer and murmured, "I know how difficult overdrinking can be for a family."

"Your *daed*—"

"I'm not talking about him. I'm talking about my husband." She swallowed hard, and her gaze turned inward.

He recognized the pose. He'd experienced it himself far too many times when he had to acknowledge that, no matter what he tried, he couldn't succeed in changing his *daed*.

"Will you tell me about him, Rachel?"

She continued to stare into her memories, and he wondered if his heartfelt words had reached her. When she spoke, he didn't know if it was in response to what he'd said, or if she was giving voice to the past's pain.

"He liked to drink beer with his friends. Sometimes too often and too much. I tried once to talk to him about it, but he told me I didn't know what I was talking about. When he was in an accident after he'd been drinking and almost died, I thought the truth might come out, but he somehow kept it hidden. I know he didn't want his boss to know because that might have caused trouble at work."

"So he wasn't a farmer?"

She shook her head. "No, but his job was everything to him."

"Not everything when he had you and your daughters."

She wore a sad smile. "Travis loved his job first and foremost."

"Travis? That was your husband's name?"

For a moment, as she stood, he thought she'd change the subject as she had so many times when he asked questions about her past. Instead she filled two cups with *kaffi*.

"Isn't that an unusual name for a plain man?" he asked.

She paused in the middle of the room as if she didn't know which way to go. "His parents must have liked it if they gave it to him." A spasm of something he couldn't define seemed to make her face tighten as tears glittered in her eyes. "They seem comfortable making their own rules." She hiccuped a sob. "Just as my *daed* did. I hoped,

Isaac… I really hoped he'd changed. That he'd want to change, but he hasn't."

"I'm sorry." He stood and put his arms around her.

She pressed her face to his chest and began to weep, as deeply and as openly as her young daughters had earlier. He guided her to the sofa. Sitting beside her, he held her as she cried for the dreams that had died in the crucible of her *daed*'s uncontrolled rage tonight.

Chapter Thirteen

It wasn't easy to be cheerful for her daughters the next morning, but Rachel did everything she could to wash away the caustic memory of last night's debacle at supper. She let Abby know she needed the day to spend with Loribeth and Eva. She stopped at the day-care center and told Gwen that the girls wouldn't be attending.

She took them to the Saturday farmers market in a parking lot of a bank across from the high school. It was the final week for the market, and she wanted to get more of the delicious apples she'd bought there. Though the day was unseasonably warm, not many people had come to the market. She was able to let the girls skip around without worrying they'd trip someone or fall over a bag of vegetables in front of a table.

Wherever she stopped, everyone was talking about the odd weather and reports of a strengthening tropical storm churning the seas to the south. Reports said the storm would remain at sea and bypass New England. That didn't halt the speculation. Vermonters always loved to talk—and complain—about the weather, but she heard the faint edge of worry in their voices. After Hurricane

Kevin's devastation last year, the residents of Evergreen Corners were more anxious than usual.

No matter how many conversations she was part of, she couldn't stop thinking of how she'd sobbed in Isaac's arms last night. He hadn't implored her to stop or soothed her with platitudes about everything being okay. He'd held her until she finished mourning what she'd never had with her *daed*. When she regained some control, he'd handed her a handkerchief and let her wipe her eyes and blow her nose. He'd squeezed her hand and, before he'd left, urged her to go to bed and leave the dishes for the next day.

She hadn't, and a few more tears had fallen into the soapy water before she'd gone into her small bedroom and her bed that seemed too large and too empty. She'd found a few minutes of sleep as the sun was about to rise, then woke the girls and began a new day.

She had to let go of old dreams and look for new ones. She didn't need to look far, because she had her beloved *kinder*. She might never be able to kiss Isaac, as she'd longed to last night before he left, but she could dream. She could…

Rachel stopped in midstep when a too-familiar form stepped in front of her. Ignoring her first instinct to run away as fast as she could, she waited for her *daed* to speak. She noticed Robert standing behind him. Her daughters were checking out some wooden toys, oblivious to what was happening, but the space was filled with merchants. Her *daed* wouldn't be *dumm* enough to try to hurt them in public.

She hoped.

When he opened his mouth, she tried to prepare herself for whatever vitriol he would fire at her. "I want to say goodbye, daughter."

She nodded, not sure what she could or should say in response. He'd used her words against her throughout her childhood.

"And to apologize."

Shocked, she whispered, "*You* want to apologize?"

"I didn't mean to scare your daughter. My temper gets the better of me sometimes." He sighed. "I told myself I wouldn't lose it when I was with you and your *kinder*, and I did keep it for a long time."

"*Danki* for trying." What else could she say? It wouldn't get her anywhere to argue that an hour in her company wasn't a long time to hold on to his temper.

"I know you never understood that what I did was in your best interests."

"You're right. I'll never understand that."

He shuffled his feet as if unsure what to say next. Did he expect her to forgive him? She had tried for years, but she'd come to realize he wouldn't be anything more than he was. She couldn't forget the horrors she and her siblings had survived.

"Before I go," he said, "I've got one question— Where have you been?"

"As far away as I could be." She wasn't going to reveal the truth to him, because she didn't trust him. Not as she wanted to trust Isaac.

He nodded, then turned and began to walk away. She was appalled when a wisp of sympathy seeped into her heart. He'd lost almost everything by not being able to keep his temper. That was so sad.

You need to forgive Manassas, Rachel. Not for him, but for yourself. Carrying around anger eats at you. Besides, as we're taught, we can only hope for forgiveness if we offer it.

Isaac had spoken the words with the clarity of his

faith. She wished she could be as sure he was right. Not about forgiveness. She understood that to be forgiven, she must learn to forgive. Was offering forgiveness to a man who had beaten her and driven her from home even possible?

It had to be. She knew that as she knew she needed air to live.

"I forgive you," she said to his back.

He faltered but didn't look at her as he continued in the opposite direction.

She closed her eyes as God's grace suffused through her. All the times she'd cried out for Him to come and rescue her, she hadn't realized that she only needed to open herself to forgiveness. She had to forgive *Daed* and to forgive herself as well, for believing on some level that she'd deserved every beating she'd received. She hadn't. She was born of God's love and worthy of being loved.

"Rachel?"

She looked at her brother, who'd come to stand in front of her. "Robert, are you leaving, too?"

"*Ja*. I must warn Arlene to keep a close eye on her *kinder*, though I think she already knows." He sighed. "I so wanted to believe *Daed* had changed that I stopped noticing how she sends them off to play with friends or do chores when *Daed* visits. She and her husband have been talking about moving to Indiana, and that may be why. How could I have been so blind?"

"Don't blame yourself for this. I was taken in, too, because I wanted to believe we could have the family we always wanted." She gripped his arm. "Robert, move far away from him and find yourself someone *wunderbaar* to love."

"As you plan to do with Isaac?"

She wouldn't be false with her brother. "Isaac wants a wife who's something I'm not, Robert."

"Are you so sure of that? I've seen how he looks at you." He gave her a sad grin. "He didn't hesitate to leap to the defense of you and your daughters. Even *Daed* couldn't be oblivious to that." His smile warmed. "I know *hochmut* is a sin, Rachel, but I don't think I've ever been prouder of someone than I was of you when you defended Loribeth." He glanced at the man striding away toward the green. "Would it be okay if I came to visit sometime?"

"Anytime."

"I'm intrigued by the work everyone is doing here, and I'd like to lend a hand." He gave her a small smile. "As a *danki* for what this village has done for my sister and my nieces."

"The projects here are planned to be finished by year's end."

"They plan to get that covered bridge fixed by then?"

"Apparently the original funds for the bridge were sidetracked to a different project. Are there more? I don't know. I don't know what's going to happen after Christmas." She put her hand on his forearm again. "Please come and visit us, Robert. I've missed you and Arlene. Tell her that."

"I will, and maybe sometime you'll come to Ohio to visit us."

"Maybe." Her gaze slid past him. "Not in the near future."

Looking over his shoulder at their *daed*, he nodded. "I understand. Let me get him home and settled, and I'll write to you about coming for a longer visit."

She embraced him. "I can't wait."

"Me, either." He gave her another hug, then turned

to follow their *daed* toward the bridge at the center of the village.

Eva slipped her hand into Rachel's. "*Grossdawdi* angry. God says be happy. I-zak says so."

"Isaac is right," she replied as she wiped her hand against the sweat on her forehead. It was far too hot for an autumn morning. "Let's finish our shopping."

She held out her hands to her girls. Eva grabbed hold, but Loribeth didn't.

"Your *daed* came to see you," her older daughter said as thick tears fell over her lashes. "Why won't mine come to see me?"

Rachel squatted in front of Loribeth, wondering how she could have failed to notice that her daughter missed her *daed* so deeply. "He would if he could."

"He hasn't come to see me." Her small voice broke. "It's because of *him*, ain't so?"

"What him?"

"I-zak! *Daed* doesn't want him here, pretending to be our *daed*."

"Isaac isn't trying to pretend to be your *daed*. He knows he and your *daed* are two different people." She doubted her daughter could conceive how dissimilar the two men truly were.

Maybe Loribeth couldn't, but she'd sensed the ways Isaac and Travis were alike. Both were dedicated to any job they took on, and worked hard until it was completed to their satisfaction. They assumed leadership roles with ease and had earned the respect of those around them. Most important, they cared about her small family.

"I miss my *daed*."

She drew her daughter to her and held Loribeth's cheek against her heart. "I miss him, too."

"You do?"

"With every breath I take, but I'm grateful God gave you to us because you're so much like your *daed*. Not only do you look like him, but you're strong and smart like him."

"So he can't come back?"

Looking over Loribeth's head, she motioned for Eva to come closer. Eva was on the edge of tears, too, though Rachel doubted the little girl understood what they were talking about. Eva knew only that her sister and *mamm* were upset.

Rachel put her arms around her daughters. Meeting their watery gazes, she said, "Your *daed* is with God, and both he and God are watching over you every day and every night. Your *daed* loved you. Don't forget that. Not ever."

The girls nodded gravely.

"Here in Evergreen Corners, Isaac is a part of our life." *At least for now.* Taking a steadying breath, she added, "Nobody will ever take *Daed*'s place in your heart."

"Or yours?" asked Loribeth, uncertain.

"Ja." She smiled as she tapped the middle of her daughter's narrow chest. "Did you know that hearts are balloons? Hearts get bigger the more love you put into them like balloons get bigger when you put more air into them. However, while balloons can only get so big before they burst, your heart can keep getting bigger and bigger to hold every bit of the love you want to put into it."

"Really?"

"Think about it, Loribeth. When we first came to Evergreen Corners, you had love in your heart for me and Eva and *Daed*, ain't so?"

"Ja."

"Then you found room in your heart for Miss Gwen and Abby and Pastor Hershey and your new friends."

"Me, too?" asked Eva.

"You, too." She put her fingers over the little girl's heart. "I can tell you've got lots of room in your hearts for love."

The *kinder* considered her words in silence, and Rachel knew she'd implanted a new idea in her daughters' heads.

Standing, she smiled. "While we're here, let's get some fresh eggs so we can bake an applesauce cake tomorrow."

As she'd hoped, the mention of their favorite cake distracted her daughters. They debated the merits of white eggs over brown eggs, though Rachel and the lady selling the eggs assured them the only difference was the color of the shells. Loribeth wanted the biggest eggs while Eva declared that the smaller ones would make a cuter cake. Selecting a mixture of brown and white eggs in a variety of sizes, Rachel paid the woman and turned her daughters toward home.

Eva ran to a nearby table and pointed at a box of tiny birthday candles. "Pretty."

"Aren't they?" Rachel smiled. "Shall we get them?"

"My birthday, *Mamm*?" asked Loribeth.

"No, your birthday is in March, and Eva's is in April. That's not until spring."

"*Mamm*'s birthday?"

"Mine was a couple of months ago. Remember? We had carrot cake."

"No birthday," Eva said, her lips trembling and great tears filling her eyes.

Loribeth looked ready to cry, too.

"I know someone who's having a birthday soon. Isaac." Rachel wasn't sure when his birthday was, but the girls wouldn't care. They wanted a birthday cake and a celebration.

"I-zak?" asked Eva and looked at her sister.

A message Rachel couldn't decipher passed between her daughters before they grinned. As she imagined an impromptu birthday party tomorrow, she hoped that Isaac would play along to keep the little girls smiling.

And her, too.

Isaac set his toolbox on the floor of the closet beneath the stairs to the apartment over the mayor's garage. It was a compromise that he and Abby had worked out. She'd wanted him to leave his tools at the building site, and he'd wanted to bring them into the house. They'd settled on the secured storage area. He'd trusted the other volunteers, as well as most of the people of Evergreen Corners, until several thefts had occurred during the building of the previous house. He—and most volunteers—toted their tools back and forth to the work sites.

When he opened the door, Abby came to greet him, as she did often. Tonight, however, she said nothing as she held out an envelope to him.

"What's this?" he asked.

"A message from Rachel. She stopped by earlier and asked me to give it to you."

He took the envelope, surprised. Why would Rachel send him a note instead of speaking to him herself?

"Is everything all right between you two?" Abby asked.

"I thought so." Had he been mistaken about what had happened at supper last night? Or after? Maybe she'd wanted him to kiss her and had been annoyed when he hadn't. He was vexed that he'd let the moment pass without sampling her lips, but he hadn't wanted to take advantage of her despair.

"She didn't come to work at the kitchen today."

"I'm not surprised."

"Why?"

He related what he'd witnessed last night.

His gentle-hearted sister's eyes were awash with tears. "Poor Rachel. But I still don't understand why she sent you a note in a sealed envelope."

"Let's find out." He opened it and drew out a single sheet of paper. His worry vanished when he saw the colored figures at the top and bottom of the page. While Loribeth's drawing resembled trees and a shining sun, Eva's scribbling was indecipherable. It might have been a dog or a car or a pumpkin. It had wheels and legs and was orange. Beyond that he couldn't guess.

He looked at the center of the page and began to smile. Rachel had sent him an invitation from her and the girls to join them for the supper tomorrow. The words *Eva wants me to be sure to tell you that there will be cake* were under the time and date.

"They're inviting me for supper tomorrow," he said. Because it wasn't a church Sunday, the few plain folks in Evergreen Corners would spend the day at the community center enjoying quiet conversation and discussing the progress they'd made on the last three houses during the previous week. Some, however, took the time to visit one another.

"So I can see." She tapped the paper.

He turned it over and read the words: *Please come. We want to thank you for your many kindnesses*. He guessed Rachel had added the words before sealing the envelope. Grinning, he folded the page and put it in the envelope for safekeeping. Tomorrow, he decided. Tomorrow, he'd ask the perfect Amish woman to marry him and become his perfect Amish wife.

Chapter Fourteen

What a difference between today and the night her *daed* had sat at the table! Rachel looked out from the kitchen and smiled. Loribeth was shy with Isaac, but she wasn't spitting at him like Sweetie Pie did when provoked. However, Eva was leaning against him, chattering about a secret she couldn't tell him.

"Big one!" the little girl said.

"Eva, don't say anything else," scolded her sister.

Eva paid her no attention as she gazed at Isaac with adoration. "I-zak, big surprise. You see. Soon."

"Gut," he said. "A surprise isn't a surprise if someone talks about it." He moved his fingers in front of his lips as if he was turning a key in a lock.

Eva copied his motion, then asked, "Know what, I-zak? Big surprise!"

Knowing that the little girl was about to spill everything including her glass of milk, which was close to her arm, Rachel shook out a handful of candles and stuck them in the cinnamon cream-cheese frosting covering the applesauce cake. She struck a match and lit them before carrying the cake into the living room.

"Birthday cake?" asked Isaac.

"Surprise!" Eva exclaimed.

"Happy birthday, Isaac!" Rachel said, trying to catch his eyes.

"It's not my—" He halted himself when he glanced toward Loribeth. Her bright smile wavered. Before her *grossdawdi* had shouted at her, she never would have given Isaac any expression but a scowl. She was warming to him. "Wait a minute! My birthday is right around the corner."

Eva ran to look into the living room. "Where?"

Rachel laughed as she put the cake in front of Isaac. "It's a saying, Eva. It means something is coming soon."

Sending the girls to get paper plates and the pint of ice cream she'd left on the counter, she said, "*Danki* for playing along. The girls saw the candles at the farmers market, and they wanted to have a birthday cake. So I hope you don't mind we're celebrating your birthday early or late or whatever." She smiled uneasily. "You know them well enough to know they don't like to wait for something like your actual birthday."

"My birthday is actually the first of November. We're just celebrating it early." He chuckled as she caught the ice-cream container as it began to slip from Loribeth's hands. When he winked at her daughters, he said, "This is a *wunderbaar* surprise. To be honest, I'd forgotten my birthday was coming up."

"You forgot? How could you forget your birthday?" scoffed Loribeth.

"Grown-ups do that sometimes when they're busy with other things," Rachel quickly replied. "Isaac has been busy getting roofs on the houses before the first snow."

"*Ja*. I've had a lot on my mind."

The twinkle in his eyes told her he wasn't talking

about the houses. She looked away before her thoughts could wander in the wrong direction, such as imagining *she* was what had distracted him.

"Aren't you going to blow out the candles?" Loribeth pointed to the cake. "*Mamm* said this was the right amount."

"Are you sure?"

She counted as seriously as a judge announcing a felon's sentence, "One, two, three, seven, six, nine, one-teen, two-teen, three-teen, ten. There are ten candles."

"Ten," added Eva, not willing to be left out as she climbed up and kneeled on her chair. She folded her arms on the table.

"That's old, ain't so?" asked Loribeth.

"Old enough," said Rachel, "to know that if someone doesn't blow the candles out soon, we'll have wax in the frosting, and that won't taste *gut*."

Two small faces turned to him, eager to sample the cake. He blew out the candles. The girls cheered and Rachel clapped her hands, then held out a knife.

"Do you want to serve, Isaac, or do you want me to?"

"You. I'm accustomed to cutting drywall, not cake."

That made Eva giggle again.

After plucking out the candles and putting them on the plate beside the cake, Rachel cut four pieces. She made sure that each girl got the same amount of frosting.

She sat as Loribeth said, "*Mamm* had a birthday."

"Did she?" His tone was as serious but his eyes glittered with amusement. "Did she have a cake with candles, too?"

"*Ja,*" her daughter said. "Four candles because it was her big oh-oh-four."

Rachel stopped with her fork halfway to her mouth

when Isaac turned his gaze on her. Seeing the surprise on his face, she asked, "Too young or too old?"

"I'd say forty is the perfect age for you right now."

She concentrated on her cake. His easy grin and his use of the word *perfect* should have been a flashing yellow light for her. She needed to be cautious and not give him the opportunity to speak about his search for a wife.

The *kinder* began to sing "Happy Birthday to You" in two different keys, but their enthusiasm was obvious, and she laughed along with Isaac. Making the girls a part of the conversation was the best course. She'd keep everything light and frothy through the rest of the evening while she avoided any chance that he might propose.

Because she feared she might say *ja* and ruin their lives.

Isaac knew when he was being given the run-around. His *daed* had taught him early how simple it was for someone to avoid a topic they didn't want to talk about, or to use someone else as a way to steer the conversation in a specific direction. *Daed* had been able to discuss everything he'd been doing without mentioning how he'd finished off a bottle of vodka and somehow made it sound as if he was relating every detail of his day.

Rachel was doing the same. Each time he tried to engage her in conversation, she found a way to switch the topic to the birthday cake and how excited the girls had been to bake it for him. The one slip she made was when she mentioned saying goodbye to her *daed* and brother at the farmers market. He listened as she explained how she'd offered Manassas Yoder forgiveness. When he told her that he'd welcome Robert on his team if her brother returned before the aid associations left, gratitude gleamed in her smile.

Yet, she'd resisted his offer to help her with the dishes, telling him the birthday boy should never have to do chores. He couldn't insist, so he sat in the living room and listened to the dishes clatter in the sink, and wondered how long she would take to finish the task.

Eva paddled into the room on bare feet. She carried something that glittered in the light from the lamp hanging from the ceiling. He smiled. There were electric lights in the apartment where he lived with his sister, too. He couldn't wait to return to a plain house, where propane lamps offered a softer light along with the gentle hiss that had been a part of his life until he came to Evergreen Corners.

"What do you have there?" he asked.

"My *daed*."

His eyebrows lowered, then he raised them, not wanting to frighten the little girl. He could see she was carrying a picture frame. Was it a drawing she'd made of Rachel's late husband?

"See?" She thrust the picture frame toward him. "My *daed* is a so-der. Look."

Isaac took the frame, turned it over and stared at the picture of a man standing next to a woman who was unquestionably Rachel, though she wore *Englisch* clothing. She held a newborn in her arms, and she was smiling, her pretty face alight with joy.

His eyes focused on the man beside her. The man wore a military uniform. It was printed with some sort of camouflage. His trousers were tucked into combat boots. Isaac couldn't read the name embroidered on his chest, but he could tell it wasn't Yoder because there were too many letters.

Who was this soldier with his arm around Rachel?

As if he'd asked the question aloud, Eva tapped the picture. "My *daed*. Cutie pie, ain't so?"

"Are you sure this is your *daed*?" He wanted to be certain he hadn't misunderstood the *kind*.

"*Daed. Mamm.* Loribeth." She touched each face as she spoke the names. "No Eva there." She frowned for a moment, then brightened. "Not yet. *Mamm* says, 'Not yet.'" She looked at him with wide eyes. "What 'not yet' mean?"

He struggled to find words to answer her as his gaze remained riveted on the picture of the *Englisch* soldier with his arm around Rachel's shoulders. After telling Eva they'd talk more later, he went toward the kitchen because he wanted Rachel to explain why her daughter believed the soldier in the photo was her *daed*. He needed her to be honest with him.

Right now.

Rachel looked over her shoulder and smiled when he walked into the kitchen with Eva in tow. Her eyes widened when he raised the picture frame.

"Why did you keep this a secret?" he asked.

"I want my daughters to be accepted among the Amish, and my past can't keep that from happening."

"Your husband was a soldier."

"An Army major." She wiped her hands. "Let me put the girls to bed, and then you can ask me your questions."

"You'll give me answers?"

"*Ja.*" She met his gaze. "I've never lied to you, Isaac."

"Just hedged on the truth."

"More that I didn't offer any information unless someone asked." She looked at the *kind* by his side. "Is it time for a story, Eva?"

The little girl clapped her hands eagerly and ran to her bedroom, where her sister was playing with the kitten.

For once, Isaac didn't join Rachel in getting the *kinder* ready for bed. He heard their hushed voices and the occasional laugh from where he sat on the sofa. He tried not to look at the photo he'd put on the table by the rocking chair, but his gaze kept returning to the happy family, which had been torn apart when her husband died.

He gasped under his breath. *How* had her husband died? He remembered her talking about an accident. Had that been her husband or someone else? He found himself questioning everything she'd ever said, weighing it for the truth.

When Rachel came into the living room, she went to the table and placed the photo facedown. He guessed she didn't want to chance anyone else seeing it.

She sat in the rocking chair and clasped her fingers. "Go ahead. Ask your questions."

"That's your husband?"

"*Ja.* He was Travis Gauthier, and he was a career soldier."

He hadn't questioned that her married name was the same as her maiden name. That happened fairly often among the Amish because there were so few surnames. Clearly, he shouldn't have assumed he knew the truth. It was time to get the facts out on the table.

"How did you meet?" he asked.

"We met after I ran away from home that last time, and I fell in love with him. He died while deployed."

"I'm sorry."

A faint smile tilted her lips. "*Danki*, Isaac. I appreciate that."

So many questions hammered at his lips, but he asked the first he'd thought of when she confirmed the woman in the photo was her. "Were you shunned after you married him?"

She shook her head. "No, I left before I was baptized. By the time I met my husband, I'd been living as an *Englischer* for almost a dozen years. Travis—my husband—was a career soldier. The Army was his first love."

"After you, you mean."

"No, the Army came first, and I knew that when I married him. He loved me, and he adored Loribeth. He would have adored Eva, too, if he'd ever had the chance to meet her. However, I knew when he was offered another deployment, he'd take it. When I developed complications before Eva was born, Travis refused to leave his men and come home." Clasping her hands together as if in prayer, she bent her head as she murmured, "He was proven to be right because he died ensuring they survived an ambush."

Her face was colorless as she raised her eyes to meet his. He wondered what she saw reflected in them. Shock? Dismay? Sorrow? He felt those things and many more he couldn't name.

A single emotion burned in her eyes. Anger. He understood why when she spoke.

"The Army sent a chaplain to the house to express the government's gratitude and sympathy at the loss of my husband. They said he died doing what he loved and serving the country he loved, as if that should wipe out any traces of our loss. They called him a hero, as if hearing that word should make everything okay. Don't you think Loribeth and Eva would trade having a *daed* who's a hero for a *daed* who tucks them in each night?"

"Eva speaks well of her *daed*."

"She's only repeating what I've told her, because she's never known him. Travis was a *wunderbaar daed* when he was home. He spoiled Loribeth and showed her off as his 'little recruit' to the soldiers in his command." She put her face in her hands. "Loribeth hardly remembers him. She used to talk about him, but now she doesn't."

"Maybe because you don't talk about him."

"I do. All the time, but only with my girls. If I were to speak about him with other folks, there would be questions. Not just from the plain people. *Englischers* would remark about how proud they should be that their *daed* died fighting for our country. I don't want his death to become more important to them than his life."

As she looked at the floor, silence oozed into the room, blanketing everything and sucking the air out of the space. It was as if a million miles separated them, though he could have reached out and touched her.

The *gut* Lord knew how much he longed to touch her, to draw her into his arms and hold her so close they could savor the melody of their hearts beating in harmony. His fingers had brushed her cheek lightly, and they longed to uncurl around her nape as he tilted her mouth beneath his.

He was on his feet and walking toward her before he was aware he'd moved. When she continued to stare at the floor, he whispered, "Rachel?"

She raised her head to meet his eyes. In her eyes were shadows left by the experiences of losing her husband, as well as the past days when her *daed* had burst back into her life and threatened to tear it apart.

"I'll understand if you want to leave," she said softly. "Please don't spread the truth. Not for my sake, but for my daughters'. They don't deserve to be punished for what their parents did."

Did she think he'd run around the village green shouting out the story like a town crier?

She stood and put her arms around him, leaning into him, as one slender hand on his neck steered his mouth toward hers. Amazed by the sensation, which was as powerful and fiery as lightning at the moment their lips touched, he didn't move for the length of a single heartbeat. Then his arms enfolded her as he explored her lips. They were as sweet as he'd dared to imagine. The soft warmth of her in his arms made his senses reel.

His breath was uneven when he raised his head to gaze into her pretty face. He'd be happy to do the same every day for the rest of his life. Because...

Because I love her, he thought to himself, though he'd tried to halt it.

He stepped back from her, shutting off his thoughts. Love had never been part of his plan for finding the perfect Amish wife. He didn't want to fall victim to love and become its *dummkopf*, as his *daed* had. But he didn't want to lose her, either.

"Rachel, I have something to ask you." He put his hands on her shoulders and gazed into her eyes. "I've been wanting to for days, and it seems now is the best time."

Ice filled Rachel's veins.

Run!

The warning burst through her head, startling her. She wasn't a coward, one to race away from challenges. She'd stood her ground while in the Army and had kept bullies from pushing her aside as an ineffectual female. She'd halted the eager hands of men who believed that, in spite of so many years of proof otherwise, women joined the military because they were desperate for a man's touch. She'd served with courage and dedication. She'd held the hand of a man while he took his last breath.

"It's late. Can't this wait for another time?" She hated clichés, but didn't want to hurt his feelings.

"I don't think so. I know this isn't the right time to do

this. It's the wrong way, but we aren't *kinder* any longer, and we don't live in a normal plain community. I can't go to the deacon and have him approach your *daed* before I speak with you of a future together."

No! He couldn't be about to ask her to marry him.

He kept going while words refused to form on her lips. "You're a *wunderbaar mamm*, not only to your *kinder*, but to that kitten. You're a great cook. I've seen how hard you work, and I admire your strong faith. Everything a man could want in a wife."

What about love? her heart demanded while her mind was shouting, *No, no, no!* He shouldn't be asking her to marry him. He had no idea who she was. If she'd told him weeks ago, they could have avoided this. He was seeking the perfect Amish wife, and she was anything but.

"Rachel, would you do me the honor of becoming my wife?" Hope warmed his smile.

Oh, God, why didn't You help me find the right words to halt him from asking that question?

She couldn't say *ja* when she hadn't been honest with him. If she spoke the truth, he'd walk out of her life and never return. Her heart shattered in her chest at that thought. She'd fallen in love with him in spite of her efforts not to. Her heart was breaking, and she must wound his. Too late, she realized by trying to protect her and Isaac's hearts, she'd made the whole situation worse.

Far worse.

Chapter Fifteen

Holding his breath, Isaac waited for the answer Rachel had given him so many times in his dreams. He'd imagined her throwing her arms around his neck with wild abandon and kissing him after saying *"Ja."* Or would she flush with pleasure and whisper the word that would change their futures forever before he put his fingertips beneath her chin and lifted her face so his mouth could meet hers? He'd pondered how she'd grasp his hands and her daughters' while they danced around in a merry circle.

That last one always made him laugh as he pictured Abby's shock at her staid oldest brother capering about like a *kind.*

Rachel did none of those things.

Instead, she backed away from him, shaking her head.

Was she saying no?

How could that be? Didn't she realize, as he did, that she would make him the perfect wife? Didn't she know that he didn't care that once she'd been married to an *Englisch* soldier? Isaac had been shocked by the revelation, but he'd set aside those feelings and asked her to be his wife.

"Rachel," he said when she remained silent, "you've got to see that we could build a *wunderbaar* life together. Your daughters are as precious to me as they are to you. I'll be the best possible *daed* I can be to them and to any *kinder* God brings into our lives. We've had *daeds* who failed us, so we know how a *gut* parent should treat his or her *kinder*."

"I know, but I can't marry you, Isaac." She edged toward the dining room as she added, "I'm sorry."

Then she was gone, her soft footsteps fading as she went to the far end of the trailer, leaving him standing in the middle of her living room. His arms, which had been filled with warmth when she kissed him, grew cold. He was overwhelmed by something he hated.

Indecision.

Should he go after her and plead with her to listen to *gut* sense? Should he wait and see if she returned? Why had she kissed him if she had no intention of marrying him?

He stood in silence for two minutes—what seemed like a lifetime—as thoughts raced through his mind, before he went to the front door. He switched off the lights as he left.

Rachel would have preferred to remain at home the next morning, but she was scheduled to work at the community center. She'd ruined one relationship in Evergreen Corners. She didn't want to risk doing the same with others, though she wouldn't have been surprised if Abby told her to leave and never return. That her friend greeted her with her customary smile suggested Isaac hadn't said anything to his sister about what had happened last night.

Why would he have spoken of it? Though Isaac fought

his *hochmut,* he was a proud man. She couldn't understand how his quest for perfection had led him to her, the least perfect woman in their community.

The rumble of voices vanished, and Rachel saw Mayor Gladys Whittaker walk in. Gladys's face was lined with strain and her lips were set in a firm line.

Without a preamble, the mayor called out, "I assume none of you have seen or heard the latest weather forecast."

Isaac spoke, as he often did, for everyone gathered there. "No, but we've heard other people talking about a storm that's going out to sea."

"It isn't."

The mayor's words hung in the abrupt quiet like the last notes of "Taps" in the silence hovering over a casket. Only instead of fading, they seemed to grow larger and more malevolent.

Rachel wrapped one arm around herself and the other around Hailee's shoulders as the mayor went on, "The hurricane, which they've named Hurricane Gail, has begun following an identical path to the one Hurricane Kevin did last year." Her gaze swept the room as her voice grew dark with despair. "It's headed toward Evergreen Corners."

No one moved.

No one spoke.

Then everyone seemed to speak at the same time.

Gladys tried to call for order.

Nobody paid her any mind.

Anxious to hear what the mayor had to say, Rachel moved to the kitchen doorway. She put two fingers in her mouth and whistled as loudly as she could. The sharp sound shocked everyone into silence.

Gladys nodded her thanks to Rachel, then said, "I

know you've got lots of questions. Let me tell you what I know. The governor has been in touch with the National Weather Service and the National Hurricane Center, as well as the mayors and town managers in this watershed. We're forewarned this year. Whether the storm remains a hurricane or is downgraded to a tropical storm, we won't let our guard down. Speaking of that, the governor asked if we could use a unit from the Vermont National Guard, and I said yes. They've got heavy equipment to keep the channel clear under the bridges, which will halt the water from being dammed and rising as high as it did last year."

"We've got some equipment here, too," someone called from the rear of the room. "Not all of the heavy pieces have left."

"Aren't you in the Vermont National Guard?" Rachel asked Hailee. The combination of the experienced workers in Evergreen Corners and the unit from the National Guard might prevent last year's disaster from happening again.

"I am, and I got an alert to be ready to be activated yesterday." She pulled out a cell phone from her apron pocket and ran her fingers along the screen. Her eyebrows rose. "Great news! The unit coming here is mine." She looked at the worried faces around her. "They're good people, well-trained. If there's a way to prevent another flood, they'll do it."

"Another flood?" asked Nina from behind them. "I'm not *dumm* enough to sit here and wait for it." She pulled off her apron and threw it on a counter, not caring that one end fell into a bowl of pancake batter.

The blonde strode out into the main room and repeated her caustic words before heading for the door. If she'd hoped to turn everyone's attention to her, she failed. Instead, the gathering began to pepper the mayor with questions about timing and the amount of wind and rain the storm forecast. It had decimated areas of Florida's east coast and was hovering over the Carolinas, dropping stupendous amounts of rain that threatened to cause historic flooding.

Rachel clapped her hands, startling the women in the kitchen out of their despair. "Let's go! We've got a ton of work ahead of us." As she turned to listen to instructions from Abby, her gaze was caught by Isaac's.

His eyes were narrowed with a determination that matched hers, but she saw the flickers of pain in those dark depths before he looked away. Somehow, she was going to have to find a way to apologize to him. Not now, though, when they had to work to try to save Evergreen Corners from being washed away.

The National Guard vehicles rolled over the bridge and parked along the village green later that afternoon. The dull-colored vehicles looked out of place beneath the bright leaves on the trees and the pumpkins sitting on the steps of many of the neighboring houses.

When the volunteers surged out to mingle with the villagers watching the guardsmen unpack their gear, Rachel didn't join them. She remained in the kitchen, making sure the *kaffi* pots were full and fresh. Later, she'd ask Hailee how it'd gone. The younger woman had left hours ago to collect her equipment so she'd be ready when orders were given.

"Rachel Gauthier, is that you?"

At the surname she hadn't heard for nearly three years, Rachel spun to see a tall, black-haired woman dressed in camouflage peering through the pass-through window. Sergeant Lorea Zabala had been under Rachel's command several times during her military career, but Rachel had never expected to see her friend in Evergreen Corners.

Fright rushed through her, but she suppressed it. Lorea was her friend. She wouldn't expose Rachel's past. At least, not intentionally.

"What are you doing here?" Rachel asked as she drew her friend into the kitchen so they could speak unobserved. An ironic laugh burst from her throat. "That was a stupid question."

"I could ask you the same, and it wouldn't be stupid."

"I live in Evergreen Corners. We moved here after Travis was killed."

Her friend's face lengthened. "I heard about that. I wanted to let you know how sorry I am, but I didn't know how to get in touch with you, and nobody seemed to know where you were."

"Being Amish and a veteran don't go hand-in-hand."

"I can imagine." Her eyes brightened. "Where's that cutie you named after me?"

Rachel smiled as she recalled the day she'd told her sergeant that her *boppli* would be named Loribeth in her honor. "At day care with her little sister."

"You've got two girls?"

"I found out I was pregnant after Travis deployed. He never met Eva." She glanced toward the door. She guessed everyone was gathered around the National Guard transports. "Lorea, I need to ask a big favor."

"Anything. You know that."

"I don't want anyone here to know I was in the Army."

Lorea's eyebrows arched in astonishment, then she frowned. "Am I hearing you right? Weren't you the one who always insisted being honest was not just the best policy, but the only one? You want me to lie to these people?"

"No, but don't mention I'm a vet." She raised her eyebrows. "I could make that an order, Sergeant."

"Try it, and see how well I'll listen to a civilian." Lorea's stern frown changed into a grin. "I'm sure you've got good reasons for your request."

"I do." She plucked at her skirt. "As you can see, I've returned to living plain, and my past and my present don't fit together."

"So who is he?"

"What do you mean?" she asked, though she knew.

"The man who's not supposed to know about your amazing career in the Army because you want him to be part of your life."

"It's not just one person. Everyone in town believes I've been Amish my whole life." She was hedging, and she could tell her friend sensed that. "I'll explain further when the storm is past. We'll make time to catch up."

Lorea looked past Rachel. "Does she know the truth?"

Turning, Rachel saw Hailee coming into the community center. "No. Like I said, nobody knows." She raised her voice, making sure it sounded nonchalant. "I assume you know Hailee."

"We've worked together before. How do you know—?" She held out her hand to the younger woman, who skidded to a stop beside them.

"I was sent to find out what was delaying the coffee." She looked at Rachel. "Is it ready? Do you want me to get the big containers?"

"You know each other?" asked Lorea.

Rachel let the younger woman answer. "We've been working together here to make meals for the volunteers who've been rebuilding the town."

"*You're* working in the kitchen? I didn't know you knew which end of a potato peeler to use."

Hailee chuckled. "You know I've done my fair share of KP, Sarge."

"Get the coffee, and then join the others to unload our supplies. We need locations to store them where they'll be safe from flooding or wind damage."

Rachel bit her lower lip as she listened. She couldn't keep from flinching when Hailee mentioned which buildings were the most vulnerable. Only when her new hometown could be left in ruins once more did Rachel realize how precious Evergreen Corners and its residents had become. If debris clogged under the bridges as it had last time, the volunteers' hard work could be destroyed.

A possible solution flashed in her head. It'd worked when she was in charge of an Army reserve company repairing levees along the Mississippi, and it might work here.

"Excuse me," she said, edging past her friends.

She heard one of them ask a question, but she didn't pause to answer. Grabbing her bonnet, she rushed outside. Wind tugged at her skirt and apron, and the air was too warm and too humid, signaling the storm was getting closer. She scanned the green. Near the gazebo that bore signs of damage from last year's flood, Gladys was talking to Isaac.

She faltered, then knew she couldn't let personal issues stand in the way. Hoping that they'd be willing to listen to her when she couldn't tell them about her past experience, she crossed the green. She waited until the mayor greeted her. Isaac's eyes narrowed, but he didn't speak.

"Rachel, I'm quite busy," Gladys said. "If what you've got can wait—"

"It can't. I've got a way to save Evergreen Corners." She tried to ignore their expressions of disbelief and launched into her idea. Keeping her eyes on the mayor's face, she watched as Gladys's skepticism became excitement.

"Wait here," the mayor said before Rachel was done. "I want to get Captain McBride and his sergeant over here, so they can hear this, too." She held up a single finger. "Don't go anywhere."

As the mayor rushed to find the company commander and Lorea, Rachel felt Isaac's steady gaze on her.

"I hope you know what you're doing," he said.

"I hope so, too." She prayed he would somehow understand she was talking about last night, as well as the hurricane. Was there any chance they could remain friends?

As he walked away when someone called his name, she knew with a sinking heart the answer was the same one she'd given him when he'd proposed last night.

No.

Chapter Sixteen

Less than a half hour later, Isaac stood in the mayor's office with Rachel and Glen Landis, the project director for the aid agencies. They were waiting for the mayor and the National Guard commander.

A television in one corner of the room kept up the unrelenting weather coverage. He glanced at the screen and saw the storm had moved farther north than he'd guessed. He couldn't keep from feeling as if they were being stalked by a great monster crawling along the coastline.

Watch over everyone in the storm's path, he prayed as he'd been doing since Gladys had first announced the oncoming hurricane.

As Rachel and Glen spoke in hushed tones, Isaac went out into the hallway. He needed something to wet his dry throat. He almost laughed at his thought. When had he started lying to himself? He was thirsty, but what he really needed most was to get out of the cramped room while Rachel was there. Every word she spoke and every movement she made reminded him of his humiliation when she'd turned down his offer of marriage. She was trying to treat him as if the conversation had never happened, but he couldn't match her poise.

He stopped by a water fountain and bent to take a drink. From his right, he heard two people talking. Their words became clear as they came closer.

"You remember the unit that saved that town in Missouri during the big floods about eight years ago?" a woman asked.

A man replied, "Of course. Their plan's part of the manual that's become required reading for flood-preparedness work." Surprise heightened his deep voice. "Are you saying an *Amish* woman has had exactly the same idea?"

"Yes, sir."

"Strange, huh?"

"Not so strange when…" The woman stopped talking as the two came around the corner and stared at Isaac.

He appraised the duo in their military uniforms. The man was Captain McBride, and the woman's name tag listed her as Zabala. She looked away, but not before he noticed a flush on her well-tanned cheeks. Though he wanted to ask why it wasn't strange Rachel's idea was the same as the one in some textbook, he didn't have a chance.

The mayor rushed toward them, talking into her phone. She waved for them to come into her office.

"There's no time to waste," Gladys said as they gathered in the small space. "Not when the new houses and the whole village are at risk. Tell everyone about your idea, Rachel."

Isaac followed when Rachel pointed out the window at the meadow where he'd joined her and her daughters after services on a sunny Sunday—a Sunday that felt like part of someone else's life. When she glanced at him, then away, he guessed her thoughts were similar.

"Who owns that field?" she asked.

"The town." Gladys's voice caught. "We'd planned to put baseball fields out there, but that got put on a back burner when our resources had to be committed to flood recovery."

"The banks on this side are higher than on the other side. Last year, debris clogged beneath the bridge until the water pressure became so strong it popped like a cork, sending a wall of water and boulders and everything else along the brook's bed."

"What do you propose we do to change that?" Glen asked.

Isaac wasn't the only one who flinched at the word *propose*, but Rachel launched into her plan. As he listened, he had to admit it was simple but could be effective if they had the time to do the work.

She suggested they dig a trench from north of the bridge. It would go past the village and into the meadow. Diverting the water would ease the power of the flow and keep debris from piling so high.

"Can your people do this, Captain McBride?" she asked.

"We'll do our best." Turning to the mayor, he asked, "Do you have a topographical map of the village?"

Gladys rushed to a file cabinet and yanked out a drawer. She pulled out a rolled page and spread it across the desk. Isaac joined the others as they crowded in to look at it, but said little as Rachel outlined her plan. He listened in astonishment as she used terms he'd never heard. Confusion was displayed on the mayor's face and Glen's as well, but the captain nodded, showing he understood every word she spoke.

"You don't have to dig too deep," Rachel finished. "Just enough so the brook will overflow its banks on the lower side. The water will pool in the field like it's a retention pond." She looked at him. "I suggest you work with Isaac. Every new foundation in Evergreen Corners was put in with his supervision."

"So," the captain said, facing Isaac, "you're familiar with construction?"

"You'll find many of the volunteers are," he replied.

"Will you help Sergeant Zabala find those with the most construction experience, Mr. Kauffman?"

"Isaac," he corrected. "Plain folks don't use titles."

"I'll try to remember that. Zabala, go with Isaac and get this going. It's a long shot, but it's all we've got."

"Sir?" asked the sergeant. She gestured toward the door.

Isaac complied, hearing the intense conversation resume in their wake. As he walked through the hall to the stairs, he glanced at the sergeant and found her regarding him with open curiosity.

"Sorry," she said, realizing he'd caught her staring. "I haven't met many Amish people before."

"That's okay. I haven't met many military people."

She laughed, then began asking him insightful questions about which of the volunteers had the most experience with earth-moving equipment. Within an hour, volunteers who knew how to run the heavy excavation machinery and soldiers were working side by side as they dug a trench into the field across the brook.

The wind began to come in uneven gusts, and rain misted around Isaac as if the air had become too humid to contain the moisture. Through the afternoon, word was passed that the storm had slowed. There might be enough time to dig the rudimentary channel to divert the water cascading through the narrow brook's bed. He often saw Rachel from a distance, always conferring with Captain McBride or one of the soldiers. He kept asking himself why she seemed to fit in with them as well as she did with the plain community.

By the time the faint rays of the sun were swallowed by the roiling clouds amid grim reports of the oncoming storm, he'd assisted in evacuating more than a dozen families from low-lying areas into the high-school gym. He'd helped board up their homes. Each time he emerged from a building, he'd eyed the increasing slice into the middle of the meadow. It led to the brook above the bridge in the center of the village. Would the ruined covered bridge survive another onslaught? They had no time to try to protect it, too.

He saw someone walking toward him and realized it was Rachel. She paused in front of him.

"We need to talk," she said without preamble.

"About your trench? It looks as if it'll work."

"No, about the questions I've seen in your eyes all day. I can see it bothers you how much time I'm spending with the soldiers."

"We're plain people who have refused to fight, but you speak their language of abbreviations and half words." He swallowed hard. "Tell me the truth, Rachel."

"I will. I've never lied to you. I understand Army lingo because four years ago, I was in Afghanistan and in charge of a transportation company."

He stared at her. Rachel Yoder, the woman he'd asked to marry him, had been a soldier?

"But before you came here, you lived in a plain community in Maine," he insisted, then wondered with whom he was arguing. Himself? "Were you honest with them?"

"No, but I didn't lie to them, either."

"How was living there possible if you didn't tell them about your past?"

"I waited for someone to ask, but they assumed I was

what I appeared to be. A widow with two *kinder* who wanted to live a plain life."

"As I did. How could I have guessed you were a... soldier?" He was having a tough time even saying the words. Probably because as he looked at Rachel standing in front of him, dressed in a simple dark green dress beneath her black apron, and with her pleated *kapp* on her head, he couldn't envision her wearing the uniforms of the soldiers swarming around the village green.

"You couldn't," she said. "That's why I wanted to tell you the truth before the storm arrives. You deserve to know why I could never marry you when you're looking for the perfect Amish wife. That's not me."

He started to reply, but she'd already turned on her heel and was walking away. He took a single step to follow, then halted himself. She was right. She wasn't what he'd been searching for in a wife. He could tell his mind that, but his heart rebelled. He gritted his teeth. He'd be foolish to heed his heart, so why was every cell in his body urging him to run after her?

Isaac had no idea how much time had passed when he stood in front of the final piece of plywood from the pile outside the community center and waited for the whir of the battery-operated screwdriver he held to stop. During the night, they'd screwed wood over window after window, a task he hadn't been sure they'd be able to finish before the hurricane's strongest winds arrived. The storm couldn't be worse than the tempest playing havoc with his gut as his memory replayed the images of Rachel's face when she told him about her past.

He had to acknowledge the courage it'd taken her to be honest with him. As well, he had to admit she'd never lied to him. She'd let him keep his assumptions.

Not wanting to think of that, he ran through the list of tasks he'd been keeping in his head, checking off each one as done. Many of the residents who'd helped in the wake of last year's flood were stepping up again.

They'd helped elderly residents near the brook move to higher ground.

They'd secured the equipment and supplies. Glen had popped into the community center less than a half hour before to announce that everything had been moved away from the building sites and onto the farm Isaac was buying. After a quick call to get permission from the real-estate agent handling the purchase, Isaac had told the construction volunteers to store everything in and around the barns.

They'd gotten the town's records out of the way. Gladys Whittaker and her staff had carried those records from the town hall to the high school. The day-care center had been relocated out of the church cellar. Sandbags encircled the library and homes. They wouldn't offer much protection against a raging flood, but if Rachel's ditch worked as everyone hoped, a wall of water wouldn't come through the center of Evergreen Corners again.

His jaw worked as he tried once more to push Rachel out of his mind.

"Isaac?"

His future brother-in-law, David, was regarding him with puzzlement. How long had Isaac been standing there, lost in thought, with his screwdriver lifted like the Statue of Liberty's torch?

"Ja?" he replied.

"We're done here," David called over the rising wind. "Abby's got drinks inside for anyone who wants them before going home."

Most of the men thanked him, but hurried in the direction of their houses. They intended to be with their families when the damaging winds and rain swept up the valley and into the village.

Isaac went inside the community center, too aware his only family in Evergreen Corners was inside. He could have… No, he wasn't going to lose himself in visions of what might have been with Rachel and her *kinder*.

The building seemed oddly quiet. He realized he'd become accustomed to the screaming of the wind outside. With the door dampening the noise, his ears rang in the silence.

He was surprised when David followed him inside until he saw David's daughter working with Abby and other women in the kitchen. Collecting two cups of *kaffi*, Isaac brought them to a nearby table.

The building quaked as a powerful gust struck it. The sound of rain against the roof and the plywood over the windows would have been loud if it hadn't been drowned by the howling of the wind.

Abby rushed to his side. "I'm glad you're inside."

"Me, too." He grimaced as the gale grew stronger. The storm must have accelerated north again. "If Rachel's idea works, we may have saved the village. If it doesn't…" He took a sip of the *kaffi*, but the strong caffeine couldn't ease his exhaustion.

"It's a *gut* idea."

His eyebrows lowered. "Nobody said it wasn't."

"Everyone else is excited about the idea. If you want to know the truth, Isaac Kauffman, I think you're afraid."

"Of another flood?"

She grimaced. "No! You're afraid of Rachel."

"What?" Maybe he was too tired to follow the conversation, because it wasn't making any sense to him.

"Okay, maybe you're not afraid of her, but you're

afraid of giving your heart as *Daed* did and falling apart as he did when *Mamm* died. You've always thought you were the stronger man because you picked up the pieces and kept us together. That was easy."

"It wasn't."

She raised one eyebrow. "It was a whole lot easier to watch *Daed* fall apart than to suffer that sorrow yourself. You care about us, but not as you care about Rachel and her girls. All you had to lose when you stepped in to take over the family and the farm was having us separated among our relatives. Oh, and your *hochmut* that you'd been there to save the day." She wagged a finger at him. "Don't tell me you weren't proud of what you'd accomplished."

"I was, but I didn't brag to anyone."

"In part because you didn't want everyone to know how far *Daed* had sunk. That was a battle you were ready to wage, but it's a whole other thing when you think of losing Rachel."

He hung his head in his hands as he leaned his elbows on the table. "I get it."

"Do you?"

"*Ja.*"

"So are you going to throw in the towel because you're afraid of a future that might never happen?"

"I asked her to marry me, and she said no."

Abby's mouth became round with surprise. "You did?"

"*Ja*, and she turned me down."

"That doesn't make sense."

He wasn't going to reveal the secret of Rachel's military experience, not even to his sister. "I know it didn't, but she said no."

"When you proposed, did you think to mention that you love her?"

He flinched at the question. Had he? He was too tired to remember.

"There's no use talking about it, Abby. She said no. She doesn't want to be my wife. Me thinking otherwise was all a big mistake."

"We make mistakes, but God doesn't. Did you ever consider that He sent Rachel to you because He wanted you to see that perfect isn't all you believe it is? Only God is perfection, Isaac. He knew that when He sent His son to die for our sins and teach us the importance of forgiveness. Perfect people don't need forgiveness, ain't so?"

Before he could respond while struggling not to surrender to the world's biggest yawn, the weather radio on the counter screamed an alarm. What worse tidings could it bring them?

"Turn it up!" someone shouted.

David leaned forward to adjust the volume, and a voice echoed through the community center.

"Tornado warning for the following locations until 5:00 p.m., Eastern Daylight Time." The man listed off several nearby towns, then said, "Evergreen Corners."

"A tornado? In a hurricane?" someone asked. "Is that possible?"

Nobody replied as the room exploded into action. Abby sent her volunteers into the kitchen to make sure the stoves were off. The door to the cellar was thrown open, and David's daughter, Mikayla, began herding the *kinder* to the lower level.

Isaac's eyes widened, his fatigue forgotten. Where were Rachel and her girls?

He spun and raced toward the door. From behind him, Abby shouted, "Have you lost your mind, Isaac? There could be a tornado coming!"

"Rachel's not here. I've got to make sure she's okay."

"She's a smart woman. She'll find a safe place."

"In a trailer?"

Abby blanched. "I forgot that."

He kissed the top of her head. "Get in the cellar with the others."

"Be careful. Please." She grasped his hand. "Isaac, you falling in love with her wasn't a mistake. It's the best thing that's ever happened to you."

"I know."

"Don't be afraid to let love into your life."

"I won't!" He gave her a not-so-gentle shove. "Go! Now!"

"I'll pray for you and Rachel and her *kinder*."

"Pray for everybody in the path of the storm."

"I have been." She gave him a quick hug, then ran to where David was standing beside the cellar door, waiting for her.

Isaac stepped out of the community center, fighting to close the door after him. His hat flew off his head. It danced in a crazy spiral. He left it. A hat could be replaced. Lives couldn't.

He raced across the deserted green. He kept flicking his gaze skyward, where the clouds contorted in agony, curling in on themselves. The wind rose, then dropped before gusting so hard it nearly knocked him off his feet. Rain drilled into his face. Leaves plastered his left side as they were stripped from trees and sent rocketing across the grass.

He reached the trailer and groaned. Only a few of its windows had been covered with boards. Through the rest, lights blared into the day that was growing as dark as night. He jumped onto the steps and reached to knock. The shrill creak of a breaking tree beyond the school changed his mind.

Grasping the door, he yanked it open. He held on to it before the wind could send it crashing against the railing.

"I-zak!" cried Loribeth as she ran toward him. She gave a frightened cry when the trailer shook with the concussion of the falling tree.

Or maybe more than one being uprooted. He couldn't tell any longer because the noise inside the trailer was almost as loud as outside. Wind and rain clattered on its metal walls, shaking it like a dog with a toy. A window in the living room had been shattered, shards on the floor and wind invading the small space.

"Where's your *mamm*?" Isaac shouted over the roar.

"Something's wrong with *Mamm*!" she cried, flinging herself against him. "In the bathroom."

Horror erupted in his mind. Had she been hurt? He scooped up the little girl and ran.

By the tub, Eva held on to her kitten, her toy bear and her *mamm*, who was sitting on the floor, her legs drawn up and her face hidden on her knees. A low, keening sound came from Rachel.

He pushed past Loribeth, then edged aside Eva and the kitten. The *kind* started to protest but he didn't listen as he kneeled beside Rachel. She appeared as terrified and cut off from reality as she had the afternoon she'd been raking leaves. Had the storm triggered what she'd called post-traumatic stress disorder?

He put a single finger under her chin and raised her face. Shining trails of tears scarred her cheeks, and she stared at him as if she'd never seen him before.

"You've got to get out of here," he said.

She shook her head and pressed her face against her knees.

"You can't stay here. The girls can't stay here. This place isn't safe."

She grasped his sleeve. Putting her face close to his, she said in a desperate whisper, "We can't go outside. Can't you hear the explosions? We'll be killed."

"You'll be killed if you stay here."

"No, it's safe here. Inside. Where there aren't any bombs."

"Bombs? You're not in Afghanistan. You're here with your *kinder*. Rachel Yoder, come back to us."

It was her name that tore Rachel out of the prison of panic created by her mind. It was her name from a time before there had been any improvised explosive devices or bombs dropping out of the sky.

Rachel raised her head and opened her eyes. She stared at Isaac, who looked as if he'd walked through a wind tunnel. The noise continued outside, but it was, she realized, the roar of the wind. Not fighter jets plowing a path for ground forces toward the enemy. A sharp sound struck the window.

Hail. Not gunfire.

He was right. She wasn't in Afghanistan. She was in Vermont. The trailer rocked, and she gasped.

The hurricane!

As if she'd said the words aloud, Isaac shouted, "There's a tornado warning. You've got to get out of this trailer."

Jumping to her feet, she wobbled a moment, but it was a moment in the now, not in the horrors of the past. She forced her mind to work.

"Blankets," she ordered.

"I'll get them." He ran toward the girls' room.

Rachel stuffed the kitten into a cloth bag. The little creature screeched its outrage as Isaac returned with the blankets from her daughters' beds.

"Where can we go?" she asked as she draped one blanket over Eva's head.

"The high school. We evacuated other families there."

He swathed Loribeth in another blanket, lifted her into his arms and took the bag with the kitten from her. As he rushed through the narrow hallway, Rachel followed. She cringed at what sounded like continuous explosions.

Thunder, she realized while she stared at the broken window in the living room. Thunder and wind. Not bombs. She must not let her memories suck her into the past. If she did, her *kinder* could die.

She fought to stay on her feet as she stepped outside. Eva was crying. Rachel could feel it, but her daughter's sobs vanished in the cacophony around them.

Isaac raced toward the school. Rachel tried to keep up, holding Eva's head close to her shoulder. The wind pushed her backward, but she didn't stop running and praying. If the doors were locked, they might not have time to reach another haven.

The wind died slightly, and she realized they'd reached the high school, which was blocking it. Isaac yanked open the door and shouted something to her. She didn't understand his words, but his intent was clear.

She stepped forward, then was shoved back again by the wind. As he set Loribeth inside, he stretched an arm out to Rachel. She gripped it. The wind pushed her away. His hand tightened on her arm, and she knew he'd never let her go.

That gave her the strength to plant her feet and drive herself toward him. She ducked as something whirred over her head. She stared at a large tornado poised along the ridge above town. Awe mixed with terror as she watched it slice through the forest, tearing trees and electric poles from the ground like a *kind* plucking tooth-picks out of pieces of cheese.

She ran into the school gym. Bending, she put down Eva. She leaned her hands on her legs as she struggled to catch her breath, but somehow croaked out, "It's coming! A tornado!"

People fled the wide-open space to a pair of doors at the far end of the gym. She grabbed her daughters' hands and followed. They ran into a locker room, then into an equipment room at the far end. Balls caromed across the floor as others sought sanctuary among the racks that held equipment and towels.

Rachel dropped to her knees and arched her body over her daughters as the walls came alive, moving in and out as if a great beast hovered on the other side. There was, for the storm was a monster ready to destroy everything in its path. When arms went around her, she drew Isaac's head into her shoulder, splaying her fingers over his skull. It was the only protection she could offer.

"Protect us, Lord," murmured Isaac against her ear. "You're our haven in the storm. We ask You to calm the winds as Your son did while sailing upon the sea. Be with Your *kinder* and hold back the storm."

She opened her mouth to add to his prayer, but the lights overhead blinked once, then went out, leaving them in a darkness so deep it looked the same with her eyes closed or open. The floor shivered beneath her, and she heard a strange rattling sound.

The roof! The wind was trying to tear the roof right off the school.

Her ears popped, and the wind's scream rose in pitch while creating a rumble she felt in her bones. Something struck her shoulder, and she struggled to breathe as the very air was sucked out of her.

Then silence.

Only for a second before the hurricane's howl returned. It was almost welcome in the wake of the tornado.

She raised her head and groaned as the motion shifted her shoulder. It wasn't broken because she could move her fingers, but breathing added to her pain. Knowing she should be grateful she could draw in a breath, she looked at Isaac. In shock, she realized she could see him. The roof over their heads had vanished. Rain struck them and washed through the blood that ran from his forehead along his face. Wind rose to another shriek, and stacks of towels rose like a flock of albino birds. He reached out to touch her cheek before they checked the *kinder* and the furious kitten. None of them was hurt.

Around them, other people were looking around. Some were hurt, but none of the injuries seemed to be life-threatening. As one, everyone scrambled to their feet to find a better place to ride out the storm.

Rachel grabbed a towel that hadn't flown away and handed it to Isaac. He wiped away some of the blood, then tossed aside the towel before they found shelter in one of the nearby restrooms. Overhead, the wind tried to batter its way into the school, but it couldn't.

When Isaac drew her head to his shoulder, she cuddled into him. Her daughters curled up beside them, Loribeth holding on to Sweetie Pie, who seemed content to stay right where she was. Someone had raided the nurse's office, and Isaac now had a bandage across his forehead with gauze wrapped around his wet hair.

"*Danki* for coming to our rescue, Isaac," Rachel whispered.

"*Danki* to the *gut* Lord for letting me get to you in time and letting us find a haven in the qym's equipment room." He grinned. "'Haven in the equipment room'?

Words I never thought I'd ever say." He grew serious again. "I'm so grateful. If something had happened to you or the girls…"

"Because of you and God's grace, nothing did. I didn't expect my PTSD to erupt in the midst of a storm."

"It's caused by something more than an accident, ain't so?" His words resonated beneath her cheek.

"*Ja*. My nightmares started the night after a roadside bomb detonated right outside the vehicle where I was riding. One of my team died instantly. Another got to the field hospital, but lost both legs and an arm." She drew up her skirt enough to reveal the scars on her calf. "There was concern if the surgeons could save my leg, but they did. However, I never returned to duty because the nightmares began invading my days, too." She looked at him. "As you witnessed."

"You shouldn't have kept this to yourself. If you'd talked to others—to me!—you might have healed."

"Maybe, but the therapists I've had said it may be with me for the rest of my life."

"If that's God's will, then it'll be so, but you need to ask the greatest *Doktor* to grant you His healing." He shifted and cupped her chin. "Do that by opening your heart to Him fully."

"I've been trying." She paused as the building shook with the power of the storm. "The episodes don't happen as often. I'm getting better, but it's slow."

"Let me help."

"You have. More than you can guess."

"So why did you turn down my proposal?"

"Because of my past."

"What if I said I don't care about your past? Would you marry me then?"

"No," she whispered.

He moved to face her. "Is it because you don't love me?"

She curved her hand along his cheek. "Of course I love you. I've tried not to, but my heart won't listen. What I was—"

"Isn't what you are now. We can go together to the bishop and have him listen to your story. He will help you reach the point where you can be baptized. Then you can bury your past."

"Not all of it. Not the *gut* parts."

"God had His reasons for giving you the path you've walked. With prayer, you can learn how to keep the memories that give you joy and release all that has hurt you."

"Is it possible?"

"Everything is possible when we give our lives and our hearts over to God." He gave her a quick smile. "Of course, as I'm saying that, I realize I want to give my heart to you. Marry me, Rachel."

She shook her head. "I can't. I know you want *kinder*, and I can't give them to you. I told you that there were complications with Eva. The *doktors* were worried I would die if I became pregnant again. I had surgery to make sure I wouldn't."

Knowing her face was aflame, she looked away. She didn't want to see his expression as she'd admitted another way she was far from the perfect wife he was seeking.

His fingers steered her gaze to his. "Do you think that matters to me?"

"You've talked about having *kinder* of your own. The perfect wife would be able to give you many."

"I'm not looking for a perfect wife."

"Abby said—"

"I'm not looking for a perfect wife because I've found one. You. What other Amish woman knows how to save a whole village by diverting floodwaters? And has two impish daughters, including one who's not afraid to throw up on my boots? And makes a unique piecrust?" His voice softened into a whisper. "Do you know where I might find someone like that who loves me?"

"I might." Joy danced through her as she realized Loribeth and Eva were listening. "However, my girls have a few qualifications for the perfect Amish *daed*."

"Do they?"

Loribeth sat. "My *mamm* needs a handsome man."

"Will I do?" he asked.

Instead of answering right away, she conferred in whispers with her sister.

Eva smiled and gave him a thumbs-up.

"What else?" He tried not to smile.

"*Mamm* needs someone to kill spiders," Loribeth announced.

"*Ja*, no spiders." Eva shivered.

"I think your *mamm* knows how to kill spiders," he said. "Anything else?"

"Ice keem!" Eva interjected.

As she laughed along with Isaac, Rachel wondered if she'd ever comprehended the true breadth of happiness until this moment.

"So it seems that I met the girls' qualifications, and you meet mine. Do I meet yours?"

"*Ja*."

As his lips found hers, his arms encircled her, holding her close as if he never wanted to let her go. She didn't want him to.

Epilogue

The farm's dirt road, with its potholes, announced the arrival of every vehicle as soon as it turned onto it. Each type of vehicle created a different sound. The tires on the milk truck spewed rocks out to strike others along the shoulder. If one of the half-dozen buggies now in Evergreen Corners came toward the house, metal wheels rolled over the loose stones and fought to emerge from the soft dirt.

Rachel came out to stand on the front porch as a car rumbled toward her home. She and the girls had moved into the tumbledown house in the wake of the hurricane. The damage to the trailer had left it less livable than the old farmhouse. Isaac would join them after their wedding.

The week after the National Guard left Evergreen Corners, Rachel shared the truth of her past with the Amish community in the village, accepted their offer of forgiveness and began working with the local bishop so she could be baptized in the spring. Once that happened, she and Isaac could exchange their vows and truly become a family.

In the meantime, they'd been kept busy working in Evergreen Corners and on the old farmhouse. Though the excavated trench had prevented most of the flooding, the damage from the hurricane's wind and the tornado's fury had left its marks on the small town.

The houses built during the past year stood, though one had lost shingles when a nearby tree brushed its eaves as it'd toppled. The main bridge hadn't had to be closed, though one of its railings collapsed into the brook. The old covered bridge had lost more boards, and there was to be discussion about whether it should be torn down or repaired by the aid agencies, which planned to extend their stays into the New Year. They'd expanded their work to nearby villages that hadn't fared as well.

None of that was on Rachel's mind as she watched the car with Rhode Island plates stopping by the snowbanks in front of the house. Isaac put his hand on her arm before she went to greet the people emerging from the car.

The white-haired woman wore a navy blue coat over khaki trousers. The man, who'd been driving, was almost as tall as Isaac. He had hints of gray in his hair that was the same dark red as Eva's.

"I'm glad you're here," Rachel said simply.

The couple exchanged a glance, uneasiness on their faces. They looked past her.

"I'm Isaac Kauffman," said her future husband when he came to stand beside her. "Welcome to Evergreen Corners."

Rachel bit her lip as Travis's parents seemed to be choosing between replying and fleeing. She'd been amazed when Bianca and Gordon Gauthier had accepted her most recent invitation to come to visit.

"The girls are eager to see you," she said and motioned toward the front door.

Her daughters emerged onto the porch. Loribeth took

her little sister by the hand as they walked toward the grandparents they didn't remember ever meeting.

"Are you my *grossmammi* and *grossdawdi*?" asked Loribeth.

"In English," Rachel said. "Remember?"

"It's all right," Bianca replied as she bent toward the girls. "I understood enough. Yes, I'm Grandma Gauthier. You must be Loribeth. You're the spitting image of Travis." Bianca wiped away a tear. "You must be Eva because you've got the Gauthier hair."

"That's me!" She put her hands on her head. "My hair. Nobody else's!"

Eva's retort broke the tension in the yard. This time, when Isaac urged her in-laws to *komm* into the house, they did, chatting with the girls as if they wanted to make up for the years of separation.

In the kitchen, their grandparents gave each girl a brightly wrapped box. Rachel watched the *kinder*'s excitement. Each girl pulled out a faceless doll dressed in plain clothing. As the girls hugged their new toys and thanked their grandparents, Rachel blinked away tears. No words had been spoken, but the gifts showed, more than any long explanations or apologies could have, that Travis's parents were okay with their granddaughters being raised Amish.

Isaac touched her fingers, confirming the connection that would last until their final breaths. He smiled, as pleased as she was that another connection—one she feared would be lost forever—was strong again. One more would be reforged when his *daed* and stepmother came for Abby's wedding next month.

"You know," she whispered as the girls introduced Travis's parents to Sweetie Pie and the latest addition to their house, a puppy named Floppsy because of his big ears, "we both may have been wrong."

"About what?"

"About perfection." She smiled at him. "Because being here with you and them today is as close to perfection as I can imagine."

Squeezing his hand, though she longed to taste his lips, she went to where Eva was trying to get the puppy to do a trick for her grandparents. She couldn't wait for his kisses, the perfect gift for a lifetime of love.

* * * * *

If you enjoyed this story,
don't miss these other books
from Jo Ann Brown:

The Amish Suitor
The Amish Christmas Cowboy
The Amish Bachelor's Baby
The Amish Widower's Twins
An Amish Christmas Promise
An Amish Easter Wish

Find more great reads at www.LoveInspired.com

Dear Reader,

Everyone makes mistakes. That's one of the earliest—and hardest—lessons most of us learn. Being forgiving toward others' mistakes and our own is one of the greatest gifts we can offer. Both Rachel and Isaac have to learn that lesson and how to accept that gift along with God's grace…just as we have to take that lesson to heart every day of our lives.

The Mennonite Disaster Service is a real organization, which was established seventy years ago when a group of young people wanted to help others. MDS volunteers, who are both plain and *Englisch*, come primarily from the US and Canada and have helped rebuild homes and lives after disasters, usually weather-related or due to wildfires.

Visit me at www.joannbrownbooks.com. Look for my next book, the final one set in Evergreen Corners, Vermont, coming soon.

Wishing you many blessings,
Jo Ann Brown

SPECIAL EXCERPT FROM

HQN

*After police officer Drew Martin loses his sight
in an accident, it takes all he has to face his ex-wife—
and the feelings she still stirs in him. But for the sake
of their teen daughters, who are struggling with some
very real issues, he'll relocate to their Chesapeake Bay
town. Together, can they find a way to repair
their fractured family?*

Read on for a peek at
Reunion at the Shore, *the next emotional and
heartwarming book in* USA TODAY *bestselling author
Lee Tobin McClain's The Off Season series!*

Sunday afternoon, Drew walked into the motel lobby, Navy at his side, feeling wary.

He'd planned to talk to Ria once she got home from church, figure out what to do about living here and about Kaitlyn's upcoming release from the hospital. But before he could have that conversation, while he'd been walking Navy, Ria had called out from the motel lobby, asking him to come to some sort of a meeting. He didn't know who would be there or what the meeting was about, except that it related to Kaitlyn.

More than anything else in the world, he wanted to help his daughter. He'd committed to stay in town for the next few months at least. But the truth was, he was a disabled stranger in a strange town, with no job. Right at this moment, going into a situation where he didn't know what to expect…yeah. He was definitely on edge.

"There's a couch two feet to your right." Ria was suddenly standing next to him, and he felt a sharp tingle of awareness. Her slightly husky voice, the flowery perfume she wore—they had always had their effect on him. Plus there was the fact that she was beautiful and didn't even know it.

Thinking of her beauty stabbed him, because he couldn't see it. Couldn't read the expression on her face, couldn't watch her tilt back her head when she laughed, couldn't look into her eyes.

The loss pressed down on him, making it hard to breathe.

He sucked in air, pushed the negative thoughts away and sat down, and Ria sat next to him. After a short, quiet bark, Navy settled at his feet.

There were multiple reasons he didn't want to stay on at the motel, but Ria was one of them. He'd have to face the fact that he was still attracted to her, but she didn't want him and didn't love him. He hadn't been enough for her when they'd married and he definitely wasn't enough for her now.

"Do you want to talk about Kait's schooling now?" he asked Ria once the meeting was over.

"You really could stay here, you know," she said instead of answering his question.

"It wouldn't be good."

There was a pause. "Sure, I guess."

He heard the hurt in her voice. Maybe it was the emotions of the day, but he reached out and pulled her closer, into a hug, patting her back and, he had to admit to himself, enjoying the way she felt there.

Which was the problem. "It's too hard to be this close together," he growled into that familiar neck, and he felt her body respond in the way it always did, moving marginally closer and settling perfectly against him.

He'd ached to hold her, and now that he was doing it, the memories flooded him. From the first time he'd kissed her, young and full of bravado, pretending arrogance but secretly afraid, to the last time, when he'd put everything he had into it, hoping to save their marriage.

They stayed that way for a moment, and then she tugged loose. "Maybe it's better if you do go," she said.

"Yeah. Listen, let's both think about this a little and then I'll give you a call." He was trying to keep his tone cool, but it wasn't working.

And it would be best to get a little distance from Ria, but that sure wasn't what he felt like doing.

Don't miss
Lee Tobin McClain's Reunion at the Shore,
available July 2020 from HQN Books!

HQNBooks.com

PHLTMEXP0720R

LOVE INSPIRED
INSPIRATIONAL ROMANCE

UPLIFTING STORIES OF FAITH, FORGIVENESS AND HOPE.

Join our social communities to connect with other readers who share your love!

Sign up for the Love Inspired newsletter at **LoveInspired.com** to be the first to find out about upcoming titles, special promotions and exclusive content.

CONNECT WITH US AT:

f Facebook.com/LoveInspiredBooks

Twitter.com/LoveInspiredBks

Facebook.com/groups/HarlequinConnection